CURSED

Sarah Ruth Scott and
Simon Robert Sinclair

authorHOUSE®

AuthorHouse™ UK
1663 Liberty Drive
Bloomington, IN 47403 USA
www.authorhouse.co.uk
Phone: 0800.197.4150

Published by AuthorHouse 01/14/2016

ISBN: 978-1-5049-9774-4 (sc)
ISBN: 978-1-5049-9775-1 (e)

Print information available on the last page.

This book is printed on acid-free paper.

SARAH RUTH SCOTT AND SIMON ROBERT SINCLAIR

The definition of cursed is damned. A curse is an appeal or prayer for evil or misfortune to befall someone, to invoke supernatural powers in order to bring harm to someone. In ancient times this was used in witchcraft or other forms of medieval sorcery. Cursed is the combined story of the Harrington curse, the curse of Zyanya following the trail of a curse that has lasted centuries and finally is revealed in a massive conclusion at the end in final chapter of 'cursed'. Never has there been a more bloody experience related as this, in the entire history of the world, as the 21st century is threatened by the past, read on if you dare.

THE
HARRINGTON
CURSE
SARAH RUTH SCOTT
and
SIMON ROBERT SINCLAIR

THE HARRINGTON CURSE

ACKNOWLEDGMENTS

I have many people to thank for this book, firstly to Gemma, Jennifer, Michael and Daniel Sutton. Friend such as Sue and Naomi Giese, Cher Thompson and many more. I also dedicate this book to Scotland as most of it was written in Scotland at the old Aberlady Inn. A special thank you to the staff there who were so nice. I needed a quiet place to write and they provided me with it. Special thanks to Rachel Day who is my editor.

INTRODUCTION

The Harrington curse goes back a few generations and affected the Harrington family in a big way, it was said that Annabelle Harrington went missing and cursed three mirrors before she disappeared. The mirrors were discovered in an attic and each given to three members of the family, it was then that horrific events took place that led to death itself. Horrible visions and blood curdling screams took place in Harrington Manor. Emma an owner of one of the mirrors, was a descendant of Annabelle's Husband John Harrington who was Lord of the Manor and the first member of the family to be cursed. John discovered that Annabelle was having an affair with the artist Ralph Bedford, so he pursued and murdered him. Annabelle went missing after discovering that she was pregnant by Ralph, it is there that the strange story begins, dare you read on! A number of crime investigators from Criminal World magazine are assigned to investigate the unusual activities of these mirrors and what lies between the deaths of one of inheritors -Gladys Harrington. One such reporter called Samantha King is desperately trying to sort her own life out and believes the answer could come from her trip to Scotland on a dangerous search for the mystery of the mirrors.

Curse of Zyanya is the sequel to the Harrington Curse as the Criminal World reporters return to investigate further activities with the cursed mirrors. This time they discover the origins of the mirrors and with danger and strange phenomenon round every corner. Ruth Ashley the psychiatric nurse is invited back to help with enquiries as Fiona and Harrison investigate a strange murder. While Samantha and Elliot travel to Spain delving into families past also linked to the mystery of the cursed mirrors. As the story unravels the team of crime reporters find themselves deeply involved in Aztec history, as a vengeful witch called Zyanya proves to be more than a match for them leading to deadly consequences. Harrison is also in danger as he meets a descendant of Zyanya called Christina who is a sadomasochist and performs strange sexual acts in order to prove her dominant personality.

THE ARTIST'S MODEL

It was a midsummer day in a remote part of Scotland somewhere between Edinburgh and N-orth Berwick near a small village called Aberlady, in a forest a man was walking on a dirt track dressed in a collarless shirt and a pair of brown corduroy trousers. He was carrying a shoulder bag and wore a hat with a brim that covered part of his face. He had a long nose and a small goatee beard, he was fairly young and probably in his late thirties although he looked older due to his appearance and harsh skin. But what was more noticeable was his large staring eyes that appeared menacing at first glance. He travelled along a dirt pathway carrying a shoulder bag and walked over a stone bridge across a stream, towards a group of rocks which were situated by a set of interestingly shaped trees. He then sat on a rock and produced a sketch pad and a set of pencils from his bag and began sketching the trees. He had been drawing for a while when a woman came walking towards him she crossed the bridge and walked up to him. She was wearing a hooded top and a pair of jeans; she removed her hood revealing a beautiful face with gorgeous large green eyes and a radiant smile.

"That's quite amazing," she said admiring his work.

"Why thank you my lady," he said respectfully.

She removed his hat and kissed him on the forehead. "My clever Ralph," she said smiling.

"Why Annabelle be careful that no one sees us together," he said concerned.

"To hell with anyone else, we are all that matters," she said laughing.

"Well you are the lady of the Manor and me a mere artist," Ralph said smiling.

"You mean John, he either abuses me or neglects me, and I don't know which is worse do you?" Annabelle said with a tone of anger in her voice.

"Annabelle my love, you deserve more than that," he said squeezing her hand.

"I have you and that's all I need, you are my true love," she said with sincerity.

"I will love you to my dying breath, you are my angel, my princess, I worship you," he replied.

With that he packed up his equipment and they walked over the bridge and towards his cottage in the woods. The cottage was surrounded by wild flowers and bushes, the cottage roof had red tiles and white walls with leaded windows and a slatted wooden door. They entered the cottage and inside was just as inviting with its wooden furniture and colourful walls and beamed ceilings. They entered the kitchen and Annabelle noticed the crockery in the sink, with dirty pans on the cooker.

"Ralph really, you might wash up occasionally," Annabelle looked at him disgusted.

"Well I am the only one here and I think why bother," he replied shrugging his shoulders.

"That's not the point, have some pride man," she said filling the sink with hot water and washing up liquid.

"Oh come on Annabelle leave it," Ralph said tutting.

But a stubborn Annabelle carried on washing up and ignored his pleas; instead he decided to make a drink for both of them. When they had finished they went into the studio, Annabelle was admiring his work, paintings, sculptures and wood carvings. He could bring anything he did to life with his artistic hands and mind; he was not just an artist but a creator who loved beautiful things. But his favourite subject was Annabelle who he sculptured and drew untiringly. Annabelle watched him preparing his art tools for the day, and then became distracted by an object in the corner of the room covered in a sheet. She looked at the shape for a while and then went to peep underneath grabbing the corner of the sheet with her hand.

"Stop!" came a loud hostile voice.

At that moment Annabelle withdrew her hand and fell backwards, she looked at her hand which was covered in blood. The sight of it caused her to pass out and she fell to the ground with a thud, almost hitting her head on a picture. When she awoke Ralph was cleaning her hand and searching for the wound which was on the thumb of her right hand.

"Annabelle are you alright?" Ralph asked concerned.

"Yes I think so, what happened to me?" she asked.

"You cut your thumb, it needs a plaster or something, let me go to the kitchen and fetch something," Ralph said heading for the kitchen.

As he left Annabelle noticed something moving under the sheet, it was something large and seemed to be very active. Suddenly a head appeared it was a snake, it appeared to have yellow eyes that were looking at her, she then noticed its fanged teeth which could have been what caught her thumb, she was petrified and froze with fear unable to speak. The snake slithered slowly towards her keeping its eyes trained on her and then opened its mouth to devour her.

As it struck out Ralph returned and it vanished as if it never existed, Annabelle passed out again and left Ralph bewildered by her actions. Again she awoke and looked at Ralph wondering if she had dreamt the entire events of the day.

"Annabelle I have dressed your thumb," he said looking at her with concern.

"Ralph what's going on?" Annabelle asked with an angry tone in her voice.

"I don't understand, I just didn't want you to see my surprise for you under that sheet," he said innocently.

"Oh really, a snake is that my surprise?" Annabelle asked.

"Snake?" Ralph said puzzled.

"Oh come on Ralph I know a snake when I see one" she said angrily.

"Mirrors?" Ralph replied.

"Mirrors?" she said puzzled.

"I have got you three mirrors which are under that sheet and I am presently carving the frames," Ralph explained.

Ralph offered her a glass of water and smiled; Annabelle had the drink and sat quietly for a while. She was convinced that Ralph was lying as the snake had appeared and almost killed her, but why did he lie to her, what was he keeping from her and was it necessary to deceive her like that.

Not long after Annabelle left still bewildered by the snake and just wanting to go back to the Stately Manor where her husband John was waiting for her. He seemed very suspicious as to her whereabouts and questioned her repeatedly he refused to give up until she admitted that she had been to Ralph's cottage. John knew that he was an artist and had many models posing for his work. But he suspected that his beautiful wife and Ralph had more going on that just art, so the next time she went there he followed her.

Annabelle met Ralph in the usual place in the woods and they went back to the cottage, Ralph had his hand bandaged up and blood was seeping out of the bandage.

"What have you done?" Annabelle asked concerned.

"Oh it's nothing I slipped with the chisel while carving the frame for those mirrors," Ralph explained.

"Are they finished now?" she asked.

"Yes do you want to see them?" he asked proudly.

"Of course," Annabelle was very excited.

Ralph uncovered them and revealed the most attractive mirrors with their wooden carved frames, three of them each looking similar and with one flaw in them a blood stain not just on one but all three frames and in the same place.

"I tried to hide those stains but they keep reappearing, I don't know why really."

"Is some of it my blood?" Annabelle asked curiously.

"Yes it is, it must be special," Ralph said jokingly.

"So I am special?" she asked.

"Yes," he admitted. "So will you now model for me?" he asked preparing his canvas.

"Yes do you want me to strip?" she asked.

"Yes please, this is for a sculpture of you, for my exhibition," Ralph prepared his paint brushes.

While Annabelle stripped naked and lay across the settee, Ralph studied her form admiring all her curves and posture. Her skin was as smooth as silk and as pale as snow, he stood watching her for a while, and then began to paint on the canvas. Annabelle relaxed but then thought about the last time they made love and began to blush, she was conscious of her body tingling with excitement and she naturally responded, her body welled up inside the more that she thought about Ralph. She tried not to think about him so that she could pose for him comfortably but her body was telling her different and she began to fidget. Ralph picked up on her vibes and he was also responding he dropped the brush on the floor and approached her; she wrapped her body around him and began kissing him passionately. She removed his shirt and kissed his chest then he removed the remainder of his clothes and made love to her. When they had finished, she lay beside him and looked into his eyes.

"I really love you Ralph," Annabelle said with tears in her eyes.

"I love you but what about John?" he asked.

"I hate him, he is cruel and hateful," Annabelle said.

"He will be angry when he finds out," Ralph said looking at the mirrors.

"So let's runaway together, tonight yes tonight," she said also looking at the mirrors.

"Are you sure that's what you want? Think of what you're giving up!" Ralph said concerned.

"I don't care as long as we are together and happy," Annabelle began to cry.

"Alright if that's what you want go and pack and we will go tonight," Ralph agreed.

A short while later Annabelle got dressed and left the cottage little knowing that John was outside; he watched Annabelle disappear into the woods and then entered the cottage.

"Have you forgotten something Annabelle?" Ralph shouted.

He had his back to John and didn't expect to be attacked, as John picked up a chisel from the table and plunged it into his back digging it deep and then twisting it. He pulled it out covered in blood and plunged it in again, he repeated this ten times until Ralph fell to the ground. He then found a pipe belonging to Ralph and lit the tobacco inside, then set fire to other items in the room. Before long the whole room was in flames then he left the cottage and ran out into the woods.

When the fire brigade arrived the studio was burnt to the ground but amazingly the three mirrors were intact the wood wasn't even singed or damaged in any way. No one could explain it. Eventually they went to the Harrington Manor and were displayed on the study wall. The servants witnessed a rough going on between Annabelle and John over Ralph so everyone soon knew about the affair, but nothing else that had occurred.

The next day Annabelle had a black eye and a bruised right cheek, she remained silent and disappeared shortly after, her clothes were missing so the servants presumed that she had run away somewhere, one maid even thought that Annabelle was pregnant as she had morning sickness, perhaps she had ran away to have the child.

EMMA'S STORY

John was said to have died a short while after Annabelle went missing, he had cut himself off from the family and hidden the three mirrors away in the attic. After this he was said to have thrown himself out of one of the top windows breaking his neck in the fall. No one could say for sure why he did this as he never discussed what was going on in his head, but the servants had their own tale to tell about how he kept speaking to the mirrors and became tormented by his wife's disappearance. John's suicide meant that according to his will his eldest sister Gladys's, being the next in line in the family would inherit the house, next in line was James and then Emma his eldest niece.

Gladys's moved into the house with Emma as she was her legal guardian, Emma's parents were killed in a car crash a few years before. Emma was already close to Gladys as she used to take her to play with another niece called Chloe in the Harrington household. John believed children should be seen and not heard and so he insisted they played in the nursery or in the garden, but the rest of the house was forbidden to them. But Annabelle used to allow them to join her in the study if John was out on business; they loved Annabelle but hated John. Annabelle wanted children but had a number of miscarriages due to the way John treated her, he wanted an heir to the estate and a figure head but hated children. Emma grew up believing that he was mad, although it was said that she in fact was mentally ill. She was said to be suffering from multiple personality syndrome or as it is known today as dissociate identity disorder, some even question whether or not this really exists in the field of psychiatry.

Gladys introduced herself and Emma to the servants and settled into the Manor, all was quiet for a few years until James came to visit with his wife Margaret. James was very eccentric and Margaret was just a puppet that James controlled, answering to his every whim like she had no mind of her own or at least that's the way she presented herself to the family. Gladys was a real lady just like Annabelle so gracious slim and elegant with an air of superiority which was different to Annabelle. Emma was a little more down to earth and definitely not a lady but could still be gracious when she wanted to. She was slim with long brown hair and big blue eyes, and in her twenties, her cousin Chloe was very much the same but with darker hair. Chloe had a child, a baby boy called Thomas she was also visiting Harrington Hall happy that she was free to roam the house.

James and Margaret were like vultures looking for things to take as they had not appeared since the death of John and knew certain things had a lot of value. Most relatives had come and gone as the will had been read and their was little left for anyone. Gladys even led them to the attic where many old things existed that were never considered nice or decent enough to exist around other parts of the house. This is where the three mirrors were propped against a beam gathering dust.

"I like them," James said admiring the mirrors.

"You may have one of them," Gladys insisted.

"Only one but they are a set," James said indignantly.

"We shall have one and Chloe can have the other," Gladys said sternly.

"But that's not fair," Margaret said looking at James.

"Of course it's fair, we can each keep one and that way they will stay in the family," Gladys looked at James then Margaret with a challenging expression on her face.

Neither questioned her but just picked up one of the mirrors and left the attic, Chloe picked up one of the others and Emma lifted the final mirror. It was fairly light considering the amount of wood round it. She was asked to take it to the study where the three mirrors once hung, Gladys then asked Albert the butler to hang it up above a decorative chair.

That night Emma heard a noise coming from the study, she opened the door slowly entering with caution; she was drawn to the mirror by the sound of a muffled voice and to her horror saw the head of a woman! The features were hidden by a dark mist and it appeared to be a severed head as it moved from left to right as if it was swinging like a pendulum. Emma was transfixed on the object then saw blood dripping down the mirror and onto the floor. She let out a scream which alerted the servants and eventually her aunt Gladys. As they entered Emma was trembling with fear and began crying at the sight that she had seen, she was eventually consoled by her aunt. But when she described the experience and pointed to the floor where the blood had landed, it had disappeared with no trace.

"Come dear you must have imagined it there are no blood stains and the mirror is like any other mirror, you are tired and probably imagined that you saw something," Gladys said smiling.

"But it was there, a head and strange voice, blood everywhere!" Emma insisted.

"Well it's gone now isn't it," Gladys continued.

Emma went to bed thinking about her experience wondering whether or not she was imagining the image in the mirror or whether she was going mad like her dear Aunt Annabelle. The following morning she rang Chloe and asked her if she had experienced anything strange with her mirror. Chloe said no and so she rang James and received the same response. That night she returned to the study and examined the mirror for herself, she was looking for a mechanism that would cause the mirror to make sounds or visions that would explain what she saw. Eventually she found something near to where the blood stain was that Ralph had tried to remove and cover up. Suddenly she felt something sharp and fell back onto the floor, she began to feel faint and to her surprise saw a big hairy spider crawl out of the mirror and onto the floor. It crept along the floor with its six feet approaching her; she began pulling her body backwards feeling blood dripping from her finger. But she never looked as she didn't want to take her eyes off the spider she had travelled as far back as the door and pressed her spine against it, in a desperate effort to find some kind of object to knock the spider away she searched around with her hands. But nothing was close she quickly looked around then back at the spider, she noticed heavy books close by and suddenly ran for her life to a book shelf and grabbed some books when she turned to grab one the spider disappeared. Lolled into a false sense of security she put the book down only to find the spider crawling up her body from her feet to her stomach. She let out a scream and picked the book up, knocked it off her and dropped the heavy book on top of it with some force. Again a servant came into the room and she pointed to the book, her arm was shaking.

"Look under there, it's a spider, it's as big as a tarantula!" Emma said her voice was quivering.

Albert lifted up the book cautiously; Emma had her eyes hidden by her hands and slowly took them away. But there was nothing under the book the spider was nowhere to be seen, not a trace just like the blood and whatever else she had previously seen. Now she believed that she was going mad who would possibly believe her now! A mirror producing images that didn't exist. The next day Gladys advised that Emma stay away from the study and get plenty of rest. She rang Chloe with her tale but as expected was not believed; oddly enough James and Margaret visited acting very strangely. Margaret with her red tinted hair and bizarre dress sense like fashion gone wrong and James appearing as if he knew everything about everything in his arrogance.

"Of course you know she's insane," James said then went quiet as Emma appeared in the drawing room.

"As mad as Annabelle," Margaret chipped in.

"What was that?" Emma asked her.

"Oh nothing," Margaret said turning her head to look at James.

"I am not mad!" Emma shouted. "Tell them Aunt."

Gladys shook her head and looked at James and Margaret.

"She is just a little upset in a new home and it wasn't long ago that she lost her parents," Gladys said in her defence.

"Oh God Aunt don't tell them that, they want me locked up in some lunatic asylum, Emma the nut case, the fruit cake, well fuck you!" Emma said and raced out of the door slamming it in her rage.

Emma lay crying in her room when she heard a knock on the door; at first she didn't answer then a knock again this time louder.

"Who is it?" Emma shouted.

"Aunt Gladys" came the reply.

"Are you alone?" Emma asked not wishing to see anyone.

"Yes dear just me, the others have gone," Gladys reassured her.

Gladys sat on her bed and hugged her tightly; Emma got up and put her head on her shoulder.

"Oh Aunt sorry for swearing and losing my temper, but they got me so angry," Emma said sobbing. "Oh child don't blame their stupidity after all you have been hurt so much, now dry your eyes and let's get something to eat," Gladys said standing up.

They went downstairs and headed towards the dining room where the servants had prepared food, soup and sandwiches. The days went by without any mention of the mirror or so called hallucinations. Emma seemed happy for a while until other events took place, this time others experienced things such as a servant and even Gladys.

Emma was looking in her mirror when it suddenly shattered, followed by the light bulb exploding. Emma was in darkness, she walked blindly across the room bare footed feeling glass under her feet. She felt around and kept walking until she hit the wall, then walked left holding the wall for support.

Eventually she could feel the door but it was locked, so she yelled loudly.

"Help me, somebody I'm trapped in this room!" Emma shouted feeling scared and alone.

Then she felt something slimy crawl across her feet, it was moving slowly and then made a hissing noise like a snake.

"Oh my god!" she shouted.

Then the door handle moved and it opened slowly, a light appeared and the figure of a man was looking at her. Emma pulled the door open and rushed out seeing Albert standing there, a sigh of relief was heard by Emma.

"Jesus thank God" Emma said.

"Are you alright Madam?" Albert asked concerned.

"Oh marvellous. Honestly!" Emma said sarcastically.

"First my mirror breaks, then the bulb explodes, I have cut my feet and something crawled on me," Emma said annoyed.

"It's not just your room," Albert said trying to reassure her.

"What?" Emma said in disbelief.

"Every mirror in this house has shattered, all but one," Albert seemed upset.

"The one in the study," Emma guessed.

"Yes and other light bulbs," Albert said. "And the clocks all went backwards, others and I saw it too!"

"Backwards, you mean you actually saw them go backwards?"

"Yes. They all stopped at 10.30. Everyone single one!" Albert said.

"I have seen the image of the woman and heard her voice, I was also struggling in darkness for a while when the lights went out," Gladys said. "You are no longer alone."

"Thank god for that, I really thought I was going mad," Emma sighed with relief.

"If you're mad then I am mad too," Gladys said smiling. "The question is what do we do with the mirror?"

"Albert take it and burn it outside," Gladys instructed.

"Yes Madam," Albert said taking it off the wall.

The next day Albert took the mirror to the gardener to burn on a bonfire, but as it stood in the middle of the rubbish, it never even caught fire instead it shot out of the fire and hit the gardener who set on fire and burst into flames. He died of severe burns later in hospital and no one could explain how it happened. Not content with this Gladys had it buried in the garden deep in the ground it was missing for days, and then it reappeared in tact on the study wall where it had been before just as if it had never been taken down.

Gladys thought that someone had dug it up and put it back, she could never believe that it was a cursed mirror, some believed that Annabelle was dead and haunted the mirror. Then one day Gladys was at the top of the stairs she shouted Emma to come to her and when Emma came she saw a swarm of wasps around her, she screamed but Emma was too late she had fallen down the stairs and when Albert and the servants examined her she was dead with her head turned round. Her neck was broken and there were no sign of wasps, any stings or dead insects. Instead Emma stood at the top of the stairs staring down at her in shock.

The police arrived and took Emma to jail then on to a mental health ward, where she remained for a while until a decision could be made as to her sanity. No one could confirm her story about the mirror or any other incident that occurred in the house her only real friend and defender of truth was Gladys who was dead. Now she had to find help from another direction. She had been to university with Fiona from Criminal World magazine maybe she could help her.

SIMPLY MAD

Emma appeared on the ward, she was very calm but weary, she seemed to be aware of her environment knowing that she was on a mental health unit. Ruth the mental health nurse made her presence known to her.

"Hello Chloe I am Ruth the nurse who will be looking after you," Ruth said in a soft soothing voice.

"Hello Ruth," Emma reluctantly replied.

"I need to ask you a few things if I may?" Ruth continued calmly.

"About my mental health condition, listening to mirrors, my hallucinations and paranoid episodes?" Emma looked into Ruth's large hazel eyes. "Look I know the jargon right, all this is in the family."

"Mental health?" Ruth prompted Emma to continue.

"Yes multiple personality or dissociative personality disorder," Emma said.

"Yes I had a friend with that. Go on," Ruth beckoned.

"Well I am not mad, but okay who gives a fuck!" Emma said admiring Ruth's shinny hair.

"Give a fuck," Ruth said smiling.

"I'm sorry it's not your fault, you're only doing your job," Emma said returning a smile.

"So let's start again Emma," Ruth said watching Emma fidgeting with her fingers.

"You have lovely long shinny hair Ruth," Chloe said looking at Ruth admiringly.

"Why thank you Emma, I was once a model but shush don't say anything!" Ruth said looking round.

"Is that why you have a lovely complexion and white teeth?" Emma asked.

"Yes I suppose so, but enough about me, tell me your story," Ruth prompted.

"Well I kept seeing a head in a mirror and an eerie voice, then I saw a snake come out of the mirror and a large hairy spider," Emma mimicked a spider movement with her fingers. "All the mirrors broke in the house and light bulbs blew up, I was so scared. I was in darkness and the door was locked, I felt something slither past my legs and feet. It sounds crazy but I felt like I was in a bog or quick sand being sucked down."

"It must have been terrifying for you," Ruth said with empathy.

"Simply mad," Emma said shrugging her shoulders.

"Simply mad?" Ruth said looking oddly at her.

"Simply mad, an unexplainable phenomenon that not only I experienced, but others like Gladys with her wasps, and she saw the head in the mirror, but then she's dead so what proof have I?" Emma said sadly.

"Did the staff witness anything?" Ruth asked.

"Albert did and the gardener was on fire due to trying to get rid of the mirror, it's like the mirror is alive, possessed or cursed it can't be destroyed, no matter what you try to do to it," Emma began to shake.

Ruth held her hands and felt her sweating palms, she could see the fear in her eyes and her anxiety, and she had seen it before with people experiencing phobias. The fear of spiders as in arachnophobia or agoraphobia fear of open spaces, claustrophobia fear of closed in spaces. What had actually induced her fear was uncertain in Ruth's eyes, but whatever it was it was real to Emma.

"Seriously do you think I am mad?" Emma asked Ruth.

"It is not for me to decide Emma, we have psychiatrists for that, you were brought here so that you would be far enough away from your home and would be able to think about things away from your district. I believe Chloe lives in Scotland have you spoken to her about this?" Samantha asked.

"Yes but she said that nothing has happened to her," Emma said.

"I don't quite understand, happened as in what?" Ruth said confused.

"The mirrors," Emma said puzzled.

"You mean there is more than one?" Ruth asked.

"Yes three identical mirrors the frames were carved by the same artist and only one belongs to me," Emma explained.

"So who has the other mirrors?" Ruth asked intrigued.

"Chloe has one and Uncle James has the other one but nothing has happened with them," Emma said quietly. " But my Uncle may be lying as he wanted me in here."

"Why do you think that?" Ruth asked concerned.

"Both he and my Aunt Margaret say I am insane and want all the inheritance," Emma explained. "They think I am simply mad."

"I see, what about Chloe?" Ruth asked. "Does she feel the same?"

"No I don't think so, we grew up together, then she moved to Scotland," Emma thought for a moment. "Can you contact her? She will be worried about me."

"Okay, let me do that for you now," Ruth stood up and walked out of the interview room to the office next door.

She tapped the number on the phone and waited, meanwhile Kathy walked in the office.

"Hi Ruth," she said.

"Hi Kathy how are you?" Ruth asked then responded to a voice on the phone.

"Hi is that Chloe?" Ruth asked.

"Yes," came a voice on the other end of the phone.

"This is staff nurse Ruth from the mental health unit I have Emma Harrington with me," Ruth said once she was certain that Chloe was listening, she then put her on speaker.

"How is she?" Chloe asked.

"A little low, but alright," Ruth deliberately restricted her information on the phone.

"Okay tell her that I am thinking about her and my mirror is active," Chloe said.

"What do you mean?" Ruth asked hoping that she would elaborate on what she meant.

"I too have seen a head, it was trying to communicate but the voice was slurred and murmuring simply mad," Chloe explained. "Quite scary really."

"I am sure it must have been," Ruth said looking at Kathy.

"I know you don't believe me, but it's the truth and I have been in darkness that was scary, the door was locked and I was alone," Chloe explained.

"Alright Chloe let me pass on your message," Ruth said terminating the conversation.

"Okay, send her my love, bye," Chloe said.

Ruth looked at Kathy for support as they were old friends and colleagues they could discuss patients at ease, they were able to share their thoughts and opinions.

"Now Ruth don't reinforce Emma's delusions and don't get too involved please," Kathy said concerned.

"Kathy I purposely let you listen to that conversation so that you would hear what I heard about the mirrors, there are three and there is something odd about them," Ruth explained all about Emma and her dilemma, then she told the full story about the family tragedy. Making sure Kathy knew the facts and could advise accordingly as the senior sister. Kathy was ten years older than Ruth who was in her early thirties and who had been through her fair share of trauma and tragedy in her life. Kathy had fair hair and was a little plump or as she termed it cuddly, unlike Ruth who was slim and beautiful. Ruth also had to come to terms with her own sexuality she once fell in love with a patient called Pamela who was tragically murdered by Ruth's psychopathic ex-boyfriend Malcolm. Kathy was heterosexual but understood Ruth at least most of the time, although some things that Ruth did appeared unorthodox at times. Kathy's life was more straight forward and unless she got involved with Ruth's affairs she lived an ordinary lifestyle.

Emma settled on the ward undisrupted until she experienced nightmares and became restless, some involved the mirrors or things associated with them. This included spiders, snakes being trapped or chased by Aztec Indians, she even dreamed of Annabelle and her violent husband.

Eventually she was visited by Fiona the reporter from the crime magazine Criminal World, Ruth recognised her and called her into the office.

"Emma said you would come," Ruth said acting a little distant.

"Yes she is a friend and once a fellow student at university with me," Fiona said removing her coat and adjusting her blonde hair.

"I wrote as accurate account as I could of you in my article 'Cracked Porcelain' I hope you believe that," Fiona said concerned by Ruth's response to her.

"Yes about the abuse Pamela and I experienced," Ruth agreed. "It was a good article."

"So how are you now?" Fiona asked.

"I am good though still wary about reporters, we also had bad press," Ruth said honestly.

"I agree not all reporters have a heart and some can be ruthless," Fiona admitted. "But Criminal World prides itself on good reporters who care for people's feelings."

"Well good for you, so do you want to see Emma?" Ruth asked not willing to divulge any more information due to patient confidentiality.

Instead Emma explained everything to Fiona from the mysterious fire to the death of John Harrington and the so called curse of the mirrors. Fiona wrote a lot of information down and promised to send someone to be with Chloe and try to protect her. Emma knew that she could rely on Fiona to help her and put an end to the curse once and for all.

"Emma we need to get you out of here and go back to the Manor, we also need to get Ruth to help us solve the mystery of the mirrors," Fiona explained.

"Will Ruth agree to this?" Emma asked eagerly.

"I can be very persuasive!" Fiona said confidently. "I have already sent Daniel Harrison one of our reporters to James and Margaret's home under cover, so just keep that quiet and maybe we can find out something there." Fiona winked at Emma in order to reassure her all was well.

Meanwhile in the home of James and Margaret Harrington all seemed quiet Daniel Harrison was working undercover as planned he had successfully set up cameras and other equipment in order to catch the couple out with their plot against the other members of the family in taking their inheritance. Attempting to take all the mirrors was the beginning of their devious plan.

As far as they knew Emma had suffered a breakdown and was on a mental health unit. But Emma had been telling the truth about the mirror and was planning to prove it somehow. She was convinced that the other mirrors were a clue to some kind of tragedy and that something was keeping the mirrors apart and at the same time something wanted the mirrors to unite. In the James Harrington household things began with the breaking of mirrors and Margaret getting trapped in a dark room similar to Emma's experience. They were being drawn to the mirror for some reason led to a face and a garbled voice, then sent away for no apparent reason.

James sat in the dining room talking to Margaret.

Daniel Harrison was close by working as a handyman; he was busy listening to James and Margaret's conversation.

"Look keep this quiet no one must know about this," James said in a low voice.

"But I did experience things such as the horrid face in the mirror and a weird voice, but it was garbled and incoherent just like Emma said," Margaret admitted.

"Exactly as Emma said, can't you see she imagined it?" James said trying to convince her.

"No James it was there as clear as I see you now," Margaret insisted.

"For god sake woman we need that inheritance, we need to prove that Emma is insane," James said sharply.

"What about Chloe?" Margaret asked

"Oh she will be easy, she can't cope with her baby, she is probably suffering from post natal depression, and don't you see it's in the bag, we have them all. All I ask you is keep a level head," James insisted.

"Fine maybe then we will be out of debt," Margaret said concerned.

"Yes the mirrors will see to that," James said confidently.

At that moment one of the butlers entered the room.

"Phone call sir, it's your niece Chloe," he said.

"Thank you Jarvis," James replied.

James stood up and followed him into the study; he picked up the receiver and dusted it off with his handkerchief then cleared his throat and began to speak.

"Hello Chloe how are you?" he said jovially.

"Uncle James have you heard from Emma?" Chloe asked concerned.

"No why?" James asks hesitantly.

"I heard that she was going back to the Manor," Chloe informed him.

"Really," James said in a surprised manner. "But I thought she was ill."

"Yes well one of them is a mental health nurse and the other is a reporter, they are staying with her," Chloe said awaiting his response.

"Well evidently they think she is normal, although I can't think why," James said with disappointment in his voice.

"Define normal Uncle, compos mentis or simply mad, those are lay man's terms a little non- descriptive don't you think?" Chloe was trying to expose her uncle by teasing him.

"So you haven't experienced anything with the mirror then?" Chloe prompted.

"Not at all, it's ridiculous," James insisted. "Why have you?"

"Yes I have seen the head, not clearly but it was there and I heard a voice it was horrible and muffled very scary," Chloe admitted.

"Well perhaps you should tell someone and let it know," James encouraged her in order to show that she was also insane.

"Oh I have someone called Samantha King, she is staying with me soon," Chloe explained.

"Oh where is she from?" James asked curiously.

"A crime magazine called Criminal World, she's a reporter like Fiona at Emma's home, it's because of these mirrors they have raised a lot of interest," Chloe said hoping he would take the bait.

"That's good tell her everything and don't hold back explain about the haunted figure and the blood coming down the mirror, the spiders and big snake!" James sounded very excited. "Listen Chloe I am being called I will phone you later bye for now."

James put the receiver down and hurried out of the study; he entered the drawing room and re-joined Margaret who was eager to hear the news.

"Well what did she say?" Margaret asked impatiently.

"She like Emma is walking right into our trap, it's only a matter of time and we will be rich," James said excitedly.

"Really, so have they kept Emma locked away?" Margaret asked.

"No. But they have reporters going there and they will prove that they are insane," James said confidently.

"They are both experiencing the same things, both Emma and Chloe," James continued.

"How very odd," Margaret said looking towards the mirror.

"So don't mention about your experiences," James advised. "I don't want you locked up."

"No of course not, but we need to get rid of the mirror," Margaret said. "It gives me the creeps!"

"Fine, we can take it to the antique shop and sell it," James said in agreement.

CRIMINAL WORLD

Criminal World is a magazine dedicated to investigating crime all over the world; the reporters and photographers gather details of crime from victims, police records and also the criminals themselves. The team take steps to ensure that the public are provided with detailed accounts of events with graphic pictures that questionably cannot be compared with any other crime magazine.

Fiona Ellington is one of the reporters who are strong-minded and a force to be reckoned, with as she immerses all her energy into finding a good story. Her life is Criminal World and anything else in life takes a back shelf including love and marriage. Although she did lose a boyfriend during her time in New York, he was shot in action.

Samantha King is a reporter who joined the team from the Australian office of Criminal World. She is courageous and determined to get what she wants despite upsetting a few people on the way. She can be outspoken using her beauty to her advantage. She is known to offend people with her bad language which she often says she's working on.

Stuart Elliot was a photographer who spent a few years as a wedding photographer and then ventured into the world photographing models. He then moved into the area of crime where he found himself actually photographing a murder as it happened!

Daniel Harrison another reporter that used to work in war zones had a history in the army and used it to help him on location in remote areas. He achieved many things in his younger life recognising an opportunity for a story at every moment. He was said to even sleep with a notepad in his bed.

Many other people worked for Criminal World of course and the main offices employed computer experts and retired scientists surprisingly enough. It was a thriving concern and the connections with other areas of expertise helped to make the magazine more accurate and credible. The World Wide Web or internet serves as a valuable asset for Criminal World in order to receive vital information for the magazine.

Samantha sat opposite Fiona sharpening pencils, organising her papers and measuring each pencil checking that each one fit into her neat box.

"Sammy what are you doing?" Fiona asked.

"Tidying up why?" Samantha replied.

"Because you're getting on my nerves must you do that?" Fiona asked aggravated by Samantha's habits.

"Sorry but I can't help it," she said continuing to measure the pencils and sharpen them even more.

"No wonder you have trouble with men," Fiona said laughing.

"Well men are just dick heads who think of one thing" Samantha said laughing.

"Oh Sammy that's a sweeping statement," Fiona said playing with her blonde hair.

"It's fucking true Fi you know it is," Samantha said taking the bobble out of her hair and looking for her brush.

"So what about Scotland, are you looking forward to that?" Fiona asked.

"Oh yes being in some creepy Manor like that fucking castle, yes of course I am!" Samantha said finding her brush and using it on her long brown hair.

"Ashley Manor will be nice and not at all creepy, besides you will be looking after Chloe," Fiona explained.

"Oh some nut job that talks to mirrors and spooks herself silly," Samantha said tying her hair up.

"Sammy she is nice and has a baby, you like children don't you?" Fiona said smiling.

"You know I don't. It's all about commitment and all that," Samantha replied knowing that Fiona was teasing her.

"You're going to Harrington Manor with that mental health nurse, I feel sorrier for you with the lesbian," Samantha was responding to Fiona tormenting her by making her own remarks.

"Oh how homophobic is that Sammy!" Fiona replied.

"I am not but from that article you wrote about her and Pamela, what was it called? 'Cracked porcelain' she deserved what she got for messing about with patients."

"I thought you liked it?" Fiona said disappointedly.

"Oh Fi I am only playing you up, Samantha said laughing. "I loved the article."

"Anyway pack for a week, I believe it is chilly in that part of Scotland," Fiona continued. "Have you read up on the mirrors?"

"Yes about the things they have supposedly seen and heard," Samantha said.

"Good we need someone with an open mind and you and Elliot will be just the right people," Fiona said confidently.

"Wait did you say, Elliot?" Samantha said frowning.

"Yes Elliot will be going too," Fiona said surprised by her reaction.

"You are fucking joking of course," Samantha said angrily.

"No we need him to get photos of the place and camera equipment as evidence of paranormal activity," Fiona explained.

"Rubbish you just want to freak me out even more, fucking with my head I call it," Samantha said clearly annoyed by the idea.

"Sammy you need to curb your language and deal with your issues with Stuart," Fiona said seriously.

Samantha went quiet which usually meant that she was sulking; she began reading a magazine which was another indication that she was upset by what Fiona had said. Fiona recognised that she had upset her.

"Sammy you're a good reporter and friend please do this for me," Fiona gave her the look that no one could resist as if she was pleading. "Please Sammy for me".

"Okay. Just for you, but if he upsets me can I have your permission to slap him?" Samantha asked.

"Yes that sounds reasonable," Fiona agreed.

"I will try not to swear," Samantha agreed.

At that moment Elliot walked in to the office, he was dancing and full of life as he approached them.

"Hello ladies so we are going to Scotland then Sammy?" He said pointing to a map on the wall.

"Yes I believe so," Samantha replied trying to contain herself.

"Just like the McGregor castle nice and creepy," Elliot was trying to annoy Samantha, and Fiona was watching her waiting for Samantha to react.

"Me and you again," Elliot continued. "Like old times."

"Elliot it was last year!" Fiona said.

"My word only a year, down them creepy corridors in a murder mystery with you my love," Elliot said laughing.

"That will do Stuart, leave her alone," Fiona jumped in.

"Like she left me alone, all over me like a rash," Elliot jumped quick as he noticed a book being hurled in the air towards his head.

"You fucking conceited bastard, don't speak about me like that," Samantha said angrily.

"Go Elliot please," Fiona said pointing to the door.

"Sorry Fi but you saw what happened," Samantha said.

"Look you can swap with me have Ruth and Emma," Fiona offered.

"The rampant lesbian no thanks I am safer with Elliot, I can handle him," Samantha said smiling.

"Ruth is a nice woman and so kind, she really is nice," Fiona said in Ruth's defence.

"Yes but it's the patient thing with Pamela, hey alarm bells and hello forbidden territory!"

Samantha said. "No offence but that's going too far, out of order."

"Sorry you feel so strongly," Fiona said disappointed.

"And Emma is definitely a fucking nutter believe me with the mirror thing, like you said we will be gathering evidence to show there is no such thing as a haunted mirror."

"Maybe, we will see," Fiona said.

"You don't seriously believe in this nonsense?" Samantha said.

"I like to keep an open mind," Fiona replied.

With that Elliot re-entered the office like a tornado.

"I'm just going to pack, anything you need Sammy, flick knife or a sledge hammer?" Elliot said laughing.

"Fuck off Elliot!" Samantha shouted.

"Isn't she wonderful, beautiful with a nice figure and a mouth like a sewer," Elliot said tormenting her.

"That's really funny Elliot, go fuck yourself!" Samantha said looking back into her magazine.

"She's at it again, moaning, swearing and giving me grief," Elliot went on.

"Look Elliot I am not apologising for anything so forget it." Samantha said not even giving him eye contact.

"Okay I can live with that I'll see you at two o'clock," Elliot actually left the room without another word.

Later they set off for the north east of Scotland near Edinburgh; Samantha remained quiet listening to Elliot's favourite classical music which eventually sent her to sleep. This was probably a plot by Elliot to keep her quiet while they travelled miles up north. When she finally woke up Elliot was admiring the scenery and driving around the smaller roads through the mountains and valleys of Scotland.

"I love the scenery, the heather and the hills," Elliot said noticing that she was awake.

"Really," Samantha replied.

"Oh here we go with the attitude," Elliot said.

"Tell me Elliot was it your idea to come together," Samantha said.

"No why?" Elliot said with surprise.

"So you don't want to fuck me?" Samantha said bluntly.

"Nothing further from my mind," Elliot said innocently.

"Like at the McGregor castle experience," Samantha said.

"Oh that again don't you ever forget?" Elliot said.

"You obviously do so was I that bad?" Samantha said prompting him.

"Look you came on to me, not the other way round," Elliot insisted.

"No I didn't how dare you, stop the car," Samantha insisted.

"What are you serious we are in the middle of nowhere," Elliot said.

"Stop the fucking car now!" Samantha said becoming rigid.

Elliot stopped the car and looked at her puzzled.

"Now get out," Samantha was frowning again.

Elliot got out of the car and slammed the door, Samantha got out the other side and they both stood for a while looking at each other.

"Right get this straight it was a mistake never to be repeated," Samantha shouted pointing her finger.

"But you came to my bed and made me feel as if I had done wrong," Elliot said in his defence.

"Only because I was scared and you took advantage of me," Samantha started pacing up and down.

“That’s bloody rubbish and you know it,” Elliot said.

“Anyway I don’t want to talk about it,” Samantha said turning her back on him.

“But you brought it up,” Elliot pointed out.

“Just fuck off,” Samantha said dismissing him.

“Look we have to work together, that means getting on,” Elliot said trying to reason with her.

“Okay,” Samantha took a deep breath. “But let’s forget the incident,” Samantha said walking towards the car.

They continued their journey to Ashley Manor saying very little to each other and then when they arrived Elliot offered to carry Samantha’s bags. Samantha refused and struggled to the door almost falling over. As she reached the door the butler stopped her and carried them in looking disgusted at Elliot, Elliot was surprised at the butler’s response as he struggled in with his own luggage. Once inside the staff took their luggage upstairs and one of them showed them into the drawing room where Chloe was waiting for them.

Samantha entered the room but there was a delay before Elliot finally entered the room.

Elliot clumsily entered the room, “Sorry I am late.” He said sitting on a seat beside Samantha.

She merely gave him a look of disgust and began talking to Chloe.

"So tell me about the mirrors, from your point of view," Samantha said in a professional manner.

Elliot looked at Samantha and then at Chloe, "No pressure of course."

"Thank you Elliot," She said frowning at him.

"Can I ask are you two married?" she asked.

"No," Samantha said shocked. "Why do you ask?"

"Nothing, you act like it that's all," Chloe said smirking.

"Me with her I don't think so," Elliot said laughing.

"Look can we get on," Samantha said obviously irritated by Elliot's reaction.

Chloe explained about the mirror "At first everything seemed normal and then the trouble started," she paused to think for a moment. "I was in the study looking at the mirror when I felt around it hearing what Emma had said about cutting her finger, it was then that as I cut my own finger, that things started happening such as seeing the image of a head that seemed to sway from left to right, then a horrible voice that wasn't at all clear."

"Muffled you mean?" Elliot asked.

"Yes she didn't even sound English," Chloe explained. "Then I heard weird noises like wild monkeys and tropical birds like I was in a jungle!"

“Strange. How did you feel?” Samantha asked.

“Dizzy and weak, I began having feelings in my body,” Chloe explained touching her body. “I saw a head swinging from the hair, it was cut off in a rough manner as the skin seemed to hang down in strands, and the voice was definitely not audible and as I said seemed to be foreign.”

“It sounds creepy,” Samantha said shuddering.

“Do you want to see it?” Chloe invited.

“Yes of course,” Elliot said excitedly.

“Come, follow me to the study,” Chloe offered.

They entered the study after Chloe struggled with the door, the door was very stiff and the door itself seemed to be too big for the frame.

“The door seems to be sticking,” Elliot observed.

“I got stuck in here, the light went out and I was in darkness I felt trapped away from my child and heard jungle sounds, then my feet seemed to sink as if they were in quick sand. I felt like I was dying I couldn’t breathe, my heart was beating out of my chest as if I were having a panic attack!” Chloe said holding her chest and her eyes widening mimicking her actions.

Elliot walked up to the mirror and gazed into it, and then he had a cheeky look on his face as he spoke into it.

"Mirror mirror on the wall, who is the fairest of them all?" he paused. "Samantha he replied to himself in a deeper voice, "She is the fairest in the land.""

"Stop it Elliot you prick!" Samantha shouted.

"It's only a mirror," Elliot said mocking her. "Are you afraid?"

"I was traumatised as a child by Snow White and the enchanted mirror, my mother thought it was the wicked queen who turned into a witch, but it was the enchanted mirror." Samantha explained.

"It was just a Walt Disney cartoon nothing more," Elliot went on.

"Not to a child," Chloe said sharply.

"I was only joking," Elliot said innocently.

"Well don't it's really not funny," Chloe said in Samantha's defence. "Fears like phobia's can seem real you know."

"Okay, point taken I will just continue admiring the mirror," Elliot said looking around the frame.

"I suppose you both want to settle down and rest," Chloe asked.

"Yes I need a shower," Samantha said.

MIRRORS

That evening Samantha and Elliot were shown their rooms, Samantha's room was opposite Elliot's and next to Chloe's room the nursery was a few rooms away. Samantha unpacked and went into the bathroom to have a shower. Elliot was in his room examining his new camera playing with the aperture and adjusting the lens. He focused on a picture on the wall, it was a portrait of a woman so beautiful and yet her eyes were sad. It was a portrait of Annabelle painted by Ralph Bedford the artist the more Elliot looked at the portrait the sadder he felt.

Samantha was enjoying her shower when she thought she could hear a voice, she stood still and listened, but all she could hear was the water coming from the shower. She continued to wash and again heard a female voice, this time she turned the shower tap off and listened. Again she heard nothing so she grabbed her bath robe and put it around her.

She walked into the bedroom and looked around. "Hello," she said baffled.

"Is somebody here?" she shrugged her shoulders. "Can't be anyone," she said to herself.

She took her make up case and removed a mirror from her bag; she then lined her make up neatly across the dressing table. She noticed that a mirror was missing from the dressing table, observing the wood that supported it. Suddenly her mirror shattered in front of her and her make up flew into the air as if it was alive. She jumped and then stood up looking around her; she put on a pair of knickers and pink pyjamas. Then returned to the dressing table to attempt to get some of the fragments of the mirror up from the table and off the floor. Suddenly the light went out and she was in darkness, she tried to move but felt splinters of glass under her bare feet. Cautiously she walked away from the dressing table feeling cuts to her feet "Ouch," she said walking with her hands in front of her.

"Elliot!" she shouted. "You better not be fucking pranking me."

She could feel something on her feet crawling around her, it felt warm and slimy, she stopped and listened. "What the fuck, okay keep calm," she told herself. "You're nearly at the door Sammy, come on it's not a snake they are silky!" Samantha reached the door and felt for the handle. "Why are all the doors either stiff or locked?" she asked herself.

She continued pulling the handle down and trying to open the door then she felt something touching her face and she screamed as the door opened and she ran into the corridor. She continued into Elliot's room, the door was open and she looked around.

"Elliot!" she shouted then heard a scream that seemed to be coming from downstairs.

She ran down the stairs leaving a trail of blood on the landing and stairs, she immediately headed for the study and found Chloe with her hands over her mouth and Elliot on the floor.

"Elliot!" Samantha shouted then knelt beside him.

"Oh God is he dead?" Chloe asked.

"No I don't think so Chloe he has just bumped his head," Samantha said examining him.

Elliot opened his eyes and focussed on Samantha, "An angel." he said holding his head.

"Fuck off Elliot," Samantha said checking a slight cut on his head.

"Is he hurt?" Chloe asked.

"Not as much as I would like him to be," Samantha said harshly.

"Well, that's a bit much," Chloe said shocked at her reaction.

"Sorry just my humour, besides I have had problems of my own," Samantha replied showing Chloe her feet. "Here help me up with him," Samantha said trying to get Elliot to his feet.

"Ouch my head!" Elliot complained.

"Get me a cold wet flannel please," Samantha asked.

"I will arrange it," Chloe said pulling the servants bell.

"So what happened?" Samantha asked. "I was examining the mirror and photographing it when I felt something hit me on the head, it came from behind me," Elliot explained.

"Well it wasn't me," Samantha said laughing. "I was too busy fighting off slimy creatures in my room!"

"Well I saw a head in the mirror and heard a voice," Elliot said. "Just as Chloe said earlier."

At that moment a servant entered the room, she looked surprised at seeing them.

"Can I help you madam?" she asked.

"Yes get me a cold compress," Chloe asked.

The servant looked puzzled at Chloe.

"A cold wet flannel, face cloth for the man's head, quickly," Chloe ordered.

"So how are you Elliot?" Samantha asked.

"Like you care," Elliot said grumpily.

"Oh that's not fair I am concerned you know," Samantha said sympathetically.

"How are your feet?" Elliot asked.

"Could be better, I need to soak them make sure all the glass is out," Samantha said checking her feet.

Two servants returned with a compress and Chloe applied it to Elliot's head then Chloe arranged for a bowl of water to bathe Samantha's feet. Some of the servants who lived at the Manor assisted them. They then retired to bed, Chloe checked on her baby before she settled down.

The next few days were uneventful then Samantha began to hear the voices again. She did not hesitate this time and dressed in her pink pyjamas she headed towards Elliot's room. He didn't seem surprised to see her and commented.

"The doors open by the way," Elliot said sarcastically.

"Elliot," Samantha began.

"Yes Sammy," he said sitting in a chair and reading a book.

"Can I stay here?" Samantha looked frightened. "Please!"

"In here with me?" he asked.

"Yes," Samantha nodded.

"Is this because you're frightened?" Elliot asked.

"Maybe or maybe not," Samantha said hesitantly.

"Oh for God sake Sammy, make your mind up, why don't you give me a straight answer," Elliot said.

"Okay I'm alright," Samantha admitted

"Okay well there is room on the chair," Elliot teased.

"Err… I don't think so, I get the bed," Samantha demanded.

"No way it's my room," Elliot insisted.

"I'm joking we can share the bed if you behave!" she said smiling.

"I know how to control myself, you came onto me remember," Elliot said reminding her of the McGregor Castle experience.

"Not that again, forget all that lets have a truce," Samantha insisted. She put her hand out to shake his hand.

"Agreed," Elliot said shaking his hand.

They both got into the bed then Samantha started making noises demonstrating that she was clearly not happy; she kept looking at Elliot and continued making noises.

"Okay, what's wrong?" Elliot asked.

"Can I sleep next to the window?" She asked smiling at him.

"I suppose so," he agreed moving over.

There was a moments silence and then Samantha broken the silence with a random comment.

"I didn't enjoy the sex you know!" She said with her back to him.

"Sammy," he said grumpily.

"Sorry I won't mention it again," she said smiling to herself.

After a while Elliot could feel her fidgeting and shaking, she put her feet on his legs and yelled "Ouch!"

"You're shaking," he said feeling her cold feet on his bare legs.

"That's because I am fucking cold," she replied.

"Oh so you're not frightened?" he asked.

"No," she thought for a moment about what Elliot said about being indecisive. "Well a little maybe!"

"Sammy give me a straight answer please," Elliot said irritated by her reply.

"You feel warm at least your legs are," she said pressing her feet against his legs.

"What was that?" she said.

"What?" Elliot asked opening his eyes.

"The bed moved and I heard something," she said lifting her head.

She turned round and faced Elliot's back, then she clung to him tightly, "I heard birds not just birds but tropical birds, does that sound silly?" Samantha asked him.

"Elliot!" she continued. "Wake up!"

"What Sammy?" Elliot was getting irritated by her behaviour.

Samantha then put her arm around him holding his chest. " You are cuddly just like a hairy bear."

"Roar!" she said teasing him.

"For God sake Sammy what is wrong with you?" he asked.

"I enjoyed the sex really Elliot," she said kissing his neck.

"Oh good!" Elliot said sarcastically.

Elliot could feel her breathe on the back of his neck, and then her hand began rubbing his chest.

"Elliot," Samantha whispered.

"What Sammy?" Elliot replied also whispering.

"Hold me," she said eagerly.

Elliot held her hand that was drifting around his chest, he really wanted to stop her hand wandering as he was tired and avoiding what he considered was her advances.

“No turn around and hold me,” she insisted.

He turned around, “If I hug you and keep you warm will you let me sleep?”

Elliot could see her brown eyes looking at him, they looked like Annabelle’s eyes so sad but kind and yearning, she was wearing her pink pyjamas but the top few buttons were unfastened revealing her tanned skin. Her hair hung down the sides of her face and her soft cheeks seemed to glow from a nightlight outside.

“Hello,” She whispered her thick lips moved with a moistness that covered both lips as she spoke, she moved closer to him her body pressed against him, then pressed her lips tenderly against his and kissed him tenderly. Elliot felt the warmth from her lips as she used her tongue to wet his mouth. Suddenly the woman that he found hard to bond with was showing him affection.

“Oh Elliot kiss me back,” she said continuing to kiss him.

“Sam?” he said confused at her advances.

“Elliot,” she said still whispering.

“Can’t you call me Stuart?” He asked.

“Ohhhh Stuart,” she whispered kissing his neck.

Elliot began to kiss her back and felt comfortable with her for once.

"Are you sure you want this Sammy?" he asked her.

"Yes you idiot I do," Samantha said pushing her hand down his shorts.

He copied her by pushing his hands down her pyjamas and stroked her buttocks, Samantha climbed on top of him unbuttoning her pyjama top and then revealing her breasts, her body tingling with excitement, she leaned over him thrusting her breasts in front of his face. Elliot cupped them in his hands and he began playing with her nipples between her fingers, she lifted her head back and gave a heavy sigh. Her skin was like velvet compared to his masculine rough hands. Samantha ran her fingers through the hair on his chest, her head moved forward again and her hair covered his face. She removed her pyjama trousers and they kissed again as she pulled down his shorts and then removed her knickers, they were getting a little more wild and hot as they made love for hours. Eventually they stopped and lay down together until they both drifted off to sleep.

The next morning, Samantha woke up first finding herself naked lying on top of Elliot.

"Fucking hell!" she said in shock.

"Morning Sammy," he said looking into her eyes.

"Elliot," she said.

"Sammy I said call me Stuart," Elliot insisted.

"Why?" she said confused.

"Because that's my name," he said puzzled.

"No, why did we do this?" she asked.

"Don't tell me you regret it again?" Elliot said still puzzled.

"No sorry Stuart I'm fine with it," she kissed him on the lips. "But you really don't understand women do you?" Samantha said.

"Why do you say that?" he asked.

"Oh God Stuart you think I didn't want you?" she said.

"You said that or at least you implied it," Elliot said.

"I didn't want commitment or complications," Samantha said concerned.

"I see," he thought for a moment. "No I don't," he was certainly confused.

"I want love yes, but as for something more complicated I mean more of a commitment; you know the trimmings, marriage and children," Samantha said smiling.

"Sammy no pressure. Whatever you want," Elliot agreed.

"You mean that?" she said in disbelief.

"Yes of course," Elliot said kissing her.

"Well I have never really been loved or understood; just because I am attractive it doesn't mean I am any more loved at least for the right reason." Samantha explained.

"So tell me Sammy what do you really want?" Elliot asked.

"To be noticed and loved not for my looks or my body, but for me," Samantha said. "After all love runs deeper you know."

"I don't know what to say," Elliot really didn't understand women especially Samantha.

"Just tell me how you truly feel, without complicating matters," Elliot said smiling.

At that moment they heard a scream, they looked at each other and then both leapt out of bed and got dressed into their pyjamas and rushed out of the door. They raced down the stairs and immediately headed for the study. They tried the door but it was locked and they could here a baby crying.

"Quick Stuart, kick the fucking door down!" Samantha shouted.

"Stand back," Elliot shouted as he stepped back and kicked at the door, with one great shove he both managed to push the door open and fell onto the floor. Chloe was holding the baby in her arms. "He's not breathing," she shouted.

Samantha took the baby off Chloe and rendered first aid, giving him mouth to mouth resuscitation, then chest compression with her fingers. Elliot held Chloe and tried to comfort her; she was trembling and trying to keep calm. Eventually Samantha got him breathing and had stabilised him, she then handed him back to Chloe.

"Thank you Sammy, you are marvellous," Chloe said holding her baby.

"Chloe what happened?" Elliot asked.

"Something came out of the mirror and landed on his face, it was like jelly but covered his face and was suffocating him," Chloe said in disbelief.

"Strange, very odd," Sammy said looking back at the mirror.

"Speaking about what happened, what is this with you two?" Chloe asked noticing how close they were. Samantha and Elliot looked at each other and smiled.

"Well we decided to get together," Samantha said smiling.

"I see," Chloe smiled

"What do you mean?" Samantha asked knowing what she meant.

"I knew it Sammy, I am happy for you," Chloe touched Samantha's arm with affection.

"Thanks Chloe," Samantha said happily.

"I bet you will have children next?" Chloe said looking at her baby.

"Hey, let's not go too far!" Samantha said laughing.

"Let's get out of here that mirror gives me the creeps," Chloe said looking across the room.

"I know the feeling," Samantha said.

They all headed upstairs and Chloe watched Samantha and Elliot enter his room

"See you later lovers!" Chloe said teasing them.

While Samantha, Elliot and Chloe were experiencing problems at Ashley Manor James had been busy selling his inheritance or the third mirror. He had travelled to a distant shop in a remote village hoping to obtain a fair price, but was offered a minimal amount. Never the less he took the money, however when Margaret and himself returned from their journey on entering the study they received an awful shock. The mirror was back and in exactly the same place as before, James looked at it and appeared completely baffled.

"Margaret!" he shouted angrily, "Come quickly."

Margaret entered the room and was equally as shocked. "The mirror, but that's impossible we just sold it!" she said gasping. "Stay there I will ring them right now."

"Wait, leave it after all they robbed us anyway," James insisted.

"You mean by not giving us enough money?" Margaret asked.

"Exactly so we keep the mirror and the money," James said watching two of the servants pass the door. "I bet they took it as a joke".

"Not everyone is as crooked as you dear," Margaret said in a serious manner.

"Someone had to have brought it back, it can't have got here by itself," Margaret said puzzled.

"Well only us two knew about it and we didn't," James said feeling around the frame.

"What are you doing?" Margaret asked.

"Looking for wings," James replied. "Well it can't just appear here like magic."

"James!" She said annoyed by his remark.

"Well isn't it obvious I am searching for any clues that it's been tampered with in any way," James said continuing to search.

"It's only a worthless mirror," she replied.

James suddenly jumped and held his left hand, he was bleeding.

"God damn it that was sharp," James said in pain. "Don't just stand there get me something to stop the bleeding!"

"What do you need?" she said looking around.

"A damp towel or something like it, from the bathroom," James said panicking.

Margaret left the room and James started feeling dizzy, he started to see a spider come out of the mirror. It crawled along the floor and then a snake appeared just as menacing. James looked across the room and saw a shotgun on the wall; he picked it up and watched the snake moving across the room. He searched the cabinet below for cartridges; they began spilling out on the floor. Desperately he tried picking them up, keeping an eye on the snake, and then the spider moved closer until it was close enough for James to see all its features, from its six legs to its eyes as it gazed at him ready to attack. It then seemed to pick up speed as it headed towards him moving onto a nearby table. James turned the shotgun around and using the butt he began hitting it and crushing its head and body, he could hear a strange high pitched screaming sound as he hit the spider several times. He also heard a crunching sound and saw slimy yellow matter coming from it. Then he noticed the snake charging at him with large fangs and a gaping great mouth, so he turned the shotgun around and shot it in the mouth. During this time the room seemed to be in a mist, this was beginning to clear, but to his horror his wife lay across the table with her head crushed and the butler lay on the floor with a hole in his head. James dropped the rifle and began yelling and then sat on the floor, Harrison and the servants stood watching him in disbelief. Blood was everywhere up the walls and on the floor, James had been hallucinating and murdered both Margaret and the butler. The police soon arrived and began questioning everyone no one was above suspicion although it was clear that James was mentally ill judging by his behaviour and the fact that he spoke about hearing voices and seeing spiders and snakes. Harrison kept quiet about the cameras and bugging devices as he wanted to continue with his surveillance of the house and mirrors.

Meanwhile at the Harrington household, Emma was experiencing more visions. This time she was subjected to bind weed which had wrapped itself around her hands and feet. She yelled out to Fiona and Ruth who ran into the room, but by this time it was wrapped around her neck and strangling her. But all they could see was Emma thrashing about on the bed and her face changing colour from red to white. Ruth grabbed hold of her and shouted.

"Emma what is it?" she said looking at her.

Just then she stopped and looked round, she noticed that the weed had gone and sighed with relief.

"Oh thank god, that bind weed had got me and I was being strangled!" she said in a serious tone.

"Well, it's gone now," Fiona said reassuringly.

"We had better stay close by from now on," Ruth advised.

"Good idea we need to bring beds in here," Fiona said. "Or at least the mattresses."

"I'm used to nightmares, but I guess you two are not," Ruth said seriously.

They arranged for mattresses to be brought into Emma's room that night and all slept in the same room.

The following day they were informed about James.

Emma relayed everything to Fiona and Ruth who were sat at the dining room table; Emma didn't appear shocked and continued having her breakfast. Harrison also informed Chloe and the others at Ashley Manor.

"Oh my God that's awful," Chloe said.

Samantha and Elliot were also at the dining room table; Chloe beckoned Samantha to the phone.

"Hi Dan how are you?" Samantha said putting the phone on loud speaker.

"Hi Sammy, I'm fine which is more than I can say for Margaret!" Harrison said concerned.

"Well the police are here at the moment, but I can say that James started hallucinating and killed Margaret and the butler," Harrison continued.

"What did he see?" Samantha asked.

"Spiders and snakes coming out of the mirror," Harrison explained.

"He smashed Margaret's skull in and shot the butler in the head, blew it apart!" Harrison explained in gory details.

“You don’t have to be so graphic,” Elliot said looking at his toes.

“Sorry but it was awful, I actually felt sorry for both of them,” Harrison continued.

That evening Samantha and Elliot were lying in bed, Samantha was wearing her pink pyjamas while Elliot wore a t-shirt and shorts. They spoke for a while then Samantha began to get nervous again and lay on top of Elliot, wrapping her arms around him. Before long she was sat on top of him and removing her Pyjama top as she had done before, she then pounced on him like a tiger after her prey. Elliot was still sore from the previous time that she laid her claws on him, making scratches on his back. She made a roaring sound and began kissing his neck, then held her head back removing the rest of her clothes. Elliot removed his and Samantha began making love to Elliot wildly and passionately, he felt very subjective as Samantha took complete control. Elliot felt a little uneasy but allowed Samantha to have her fun, he did enjoy the experience but something was wrong. As she tilted her head back and gave her usual sigh, she brought her head forward and her head was replaced by Annabelle’s decapitated head. The face was the one on the painting but her eyes were evil and yellow, there was also blood on her neck. Elliot yelled out and pushed her away, he then fell on the floor and began gasping for breath.

“For fuck sake Stuart!” Samantha shouted. “Jesus fucking Christ!”

Elliot was almost blue and still gasping for breath, he was hardly breathing when Samantha realised he was having an asthma attack. She rushed to the bedside table by Elliot and opened the drawer looking for his Ventolin inhaler; a few other items came out of the drawer too.

"Where the fuck is it? She continued frantically searching until she realised it was in his trouser pocket. She raced back to him and opened his mouth and pushed it in squeezing the top to release the spray. "Breathe for fuck sake!" she said spraying again.

Elliot started to breathe still staring at the ceiling.

"Come on Elliot speak to me," Samantha said anxiously.

Samantha felt helpless but continued to attempt to get a response, she continued yelling at him.

"Stuart come on please," she said repeatedly then slapped his face hard.

"Oh God Sammy," Elliot said.

Samantha smiled and said, "Thank God, are you ok?"

"Yes but why did you slap me?" Elliot asked holding his cheek.

"Two reasons, one you knocked me off the bed and the other, in order to make you respond, oh and I am still trying to think of a third reason!" she said smiling.

"I saw a severed head on your shoulders," he looked around at Annabelle's painting. "It was her!"

"Oh how horrid," Samantha said frowning.

"But her eyes were horrible and evil," Elliot said. "Unlike your lovely eyes."

"Oh my poor Stuart, in that case I am sorry," she said feeling guilty for slapping him.

"Yes well you can certainly slap!" Elliot said smiling.

"I had tough brothers who taught me to fight," she replied hugging him then, realised they were still naked. "Oh look at us," she said smiling back.

"Shall we try again," Samantha said kissing him on the lips.

"You bet lover girl!" Elliot replied eagerly.

The next morning Samantha and Elliot sat at the dining room table with Chloe and her baby sat opposite, Chloe was breast feeding the baby. Elliot seemed a little uncomfortable with this; although he had seen her do it many times it did rather put him off his porridge.

"Did you sleep well?" Chloe asked.

"Oh yes thank you," Samantha replied kicking Elliot under the table.

"Yes thank you." Elliot said and smiled at Samantha.

"Very comfortable and cosy," Samantha smiled back like a love struck teenager.

Chloe couldn't help noticing a scratch on Elliot's right cheek and a bruise on Samantha's forehead.

"Are you sure you two slept?" she asked suspecting activity in the bedroom.

"Oh yes I'm sure!" Elliot said unsure exactly what she was referring to.

Samantha realised straight away as she had looked in the mirror and seen her bruise, she also noticed the scratch on Elliot's cheek. She gave a smile to Chloe and began playing with her hair then tucked it behind her ears in order to eat her breakfast.

"Mm mm coffee delicious," she said sipping from the cup. "I love a nice cup of coffee."

Samantha seemed to be over emphasising her enjoyment for her drink and teasing Elliot by removing her shoe and playing with his leg with her foot. Then sending her bare foot up his leg which was easy from her position at the table, Elliot just smiled not knowing how to respond. He was about to drink when Samantha reached a vulnerable area making him jump.

"Oh Stuart did you miss your mouth?" she said laughing.

"Of course it's all in the beans," Chloe said also laughing.

"Obviously, go for the best I say choose the best and hit the right market, where it counts," Samantha continued teasing Elliot. "Isn't that right Stuart?"

"You sound like a bloody coffee commercial Sammy," Elliot said fidgeting.

They were interrupted by the phone ringing, Chloe walked over and picked up the receiver, and she remembered to put it on speaker.

"Hello Ashley Manor," she said politely.

"Is that Chloe?" Harrison asked eagerly.

"Yes what's wrong," Chloe said noticing his anxious tone.

"I have spoken to Fiona and Ruth they suggest we get these mirrors together and find out if there is some truth about a message," Harrison said eagerly awaiting her response.

"I don't know what does Emma say?" Chloe asked.

"She is in agreement but she said it's up to you" Harrison replied.

"I agree there is something in what you say, but I am concerned something may go wrong," Chloe said concerned.

"I say do it Chloe we need answers and who knows what we may find," Samantha said looking at Elliot for support.

"Well we can't just sit here wiggling our thumbs, let's see what happens, besides enough has happened what else can go wrong," Elliot said looking back at Samantha.

"Okay I'll head for Harrington Manor at around midday see you on route," Harrison said.

"See you on the road Dan," Elliot said. "Drive carefully."

"As usual Stuart," Harrison replied.

Chloe replaced the phone on the receiver and returned to the table, she was about to eat her toast when the phone rang again.

"Hello Ashley Manor," She said a little abruptly, putting the phone on speaker.

"Chloe this is Fiona are you all there?" Fiona asked.

"Yes all having breakfast," she said continuing to eat her toast.

"Oh sorry, but I need to know about the mirrors," Fiona said concerned.

"Daniel has just rang and mentioned it, we are all meeting at Harrington Manor where it all began," Chloe explained.

"Good see you here later," Fiona said. "How's your baby?"

"Sammy is holding him, she has got used to his vomiting and smelly nappies," Chloe said laughing.

"That's amazing for Sammy!" Fiona said laughing.

"I still don't want any," Samantha shouted to Fiona. "Not that he isn't cute."

"Watch this space Sammy," Fiona said. "See you all soon."

By midday Harrison was ready to depart; he put the mirror in the boot of his car with no resistance and started on his journey to Harrington Manor. He was driving at a fairly fast pace listening to the radio when he heard a loud scream which seemed to be coming from behind him possibly from the boot of the car. He ignored it and carried on driving thinking he may have still been tired from the night before, he then heard the sound of hissing and saw a snake in the passenger seat. He tried to slow down so that he could sort out the snake but instead he was taken by surprise as it attempted to bite him. Harrison swerved in the road a few times then slowed down, but landed in a ditch as he swerved a third time. His head hit the door and then he slumped forward. He must have been there for a time unconscious when Elliot pulled up in his car; he and Samantha rushed to Harrison's car.

"Dan are you alright?" Elliot shouted.

"Dan can you here us?" Samantha asked.

"Yes. I am," Harrison said holding his head. "Help me out of this thing."

Both Samantha and Elliot helped walk Harrison away from the car, and then they helped him sit down by a grass bank.

"The mirror." he shouted.

Samantha walked towards the car, suddenly it exploded and she was thrown in mid air and landed by a tree, she was motionless her body was limp and lifeless.

"Sammy!" Elliot shouted. "Oh no!"

He raced towards her not knowing what to expect as he lifted her head up and watched her eyes open.

"What the fuck!" Samantha exclaimed.

"God are you alright?" Elliot asked.

"Ouch my head," Samantha said holding the back of her head.

"God you flew about fifty feet in the air!" Elliot said knowing he was exaggerating.

"Get me up," Samantha insisted.

Elliot helped her back to Harrison who was still dazed, they sat for a while then Harrison remembered the mirror.

"I bet the mirrors gone now," he said disappointed.

Elliot walked towards the car, and then cautiously opened what was left of the boot.

To his surprise the mirror was in tact, so he tried to extract it from the boot. The others heard a great shout and a cry of pain as Elliot grabbed the painting.

"Elliot!" Samantha shouted.

"God damn it, I've burnt my hands," he shouted.

"Stuart you might have known that would be hot," Harrison shouted.

"Stuart you fool," Samantha said rushing to him.

Harrison found the strength to go to Elliot's car for a fire extinguisher and a bottle of water. He passed Samantha the water and bandages and then headed to his car with the fire extinguisher. He sprayed the mirror then wrapped a blanket around it, then picked it up and carried it to Elliot's car. Samantha and Elliot struggled to the car and sat in the back seat together. Harrison drove the car heading for the main road to Harrington Manor. They continued to hear banging and shouting now they had two mirrors. They were a mile away from Harrington Manor when a woman appeared at the roadside she was young and beautiful wearing a hooded coat.

"Can I help you?" Harrison asked.

"Yes could you take me to Harrington Manor?" she asked.

"Of course get in," Harrison offered.

Harrison glanced at her in disbelief then concentrated on the road, Elliot and Samantha remained quiet.

"Are you going to visit there?" Harrison asked.

"No I live there," she replied.

"I thought Emma lived there," Harrison said finding it strange that the others were quiet.

"Yes she does now and so do many others," the woman said.

"May I ask who you are," Harrison asked.

"I am the one you seek and the one you wish to free," the woman said mysteriously.

"I don't understand," Harrison asked suddenly feeling very cold.

"Put the mirrors together and you will find out," she said. "The answer is in the mirrors."

"I really don't get it. You want us to bring them together?" Harrison said.

"Stop, I will walk from here," she said.

Harrison opened the door and the woman walked into the woods then vanished.

"Jesus Dan!" Elliot shouted.

"What's wrong?" Elliot asked.

"That woman did you know who she was?" Elliot asked.

"A hitchhiker," Harrison said surprised at Elliot's behaviour.

"It was Annabelle!" Elliot said shaking.

"Are you sure?" Harrison said smirking.

"Oh yes it was her didn't you notice her neck was bloody and her voice a little strange?" Elliot said nervously.

"Yes but I didn't think it was Annabelle," he replied unperturbed.

"A ghost has been travelling with us, I don't believe it," Elliot said looking at Samantha who was asleep.

Two of the mirrors were placed in the library temporarily until they could be united with the other mirror in the study, but while they were sorting this out Samantha decided to enter the study looking for Fiona. Instead she saw Ruth sat at a table reading one of the many books out of the book cabinet.

"Where's Fiona?" she asked.

"I don't know," Ruth replied sensing hostility in Samantha's voice.

"No of course you don't," Samantha said sarcastically.

"What's that supposed to mean?" Ruth asked.

"Nothing, I mean you haven't tried to make a pass at her then?" Samantha said. "I mean she is pretty."

"Look just because she's pretty it doesn't mean I am going to fancy her!" Ruth said in her own defence.

"She's blonde like Pamela, but she's straight shame isn't it," Samantha said rudely.

"Look just because I am a lesbian it doesn't mean I like every beautiful woman," Ruth said angrily. At that moment the mirror began to glow and blood poured down it. But Samantha and Ruth were that busy arguing they hadn't noticed any activity.

"Why have you got to knock gay people? Ruth asked.

"It's you I don't like, my God you think you invented sex especially lesbianism."

"I stand up for my own kind, what's wrong with that? Ruth asked.

"No you flaunt it and throw it in people's faces, both you and Pamela did that on those fashion shows," Samantha said in disgust.

"Just because it was on television and radio, we were hounded by the press," Ruth explained.

"Fucking exhibitionism if you ask me," Samantha said.

"Not at all everyone was against us, we merely defended ourselves, against religion and political extremists," Ruth replied. "We had to challenge them".

“No you didn’t, that’s a lame excuse,” Samantha said beginning to pace up and down.

“So you think the likes of priests are perfect, those who abuse young boys, they are so fucking untouchable, so righteous,” Ruth was getting angry.

“How can you say that?” Samantha asked.

“Why don’t you read the papers or magazines?” Ruth said pointing to a newspaper on the table.

“I do, they are inaccurate and lie to sell the paper,” Samantha said folding her arms in defence.

“Like Criminal World, I mean you as a crime reporter?” Ruth was referring to all reporters not just Criminal World’s staff.

“Just keep your lesbian ideas to yourself” Samantha said looking away from her.

“What are you afraid of?” Ruth asked.

“Nothing,” Samantha replied swiftly.

“Yes you are that’s why your against me, you’re frightened of something, perhaps things that you don’t know about,” Ruth said realising that what Samantha was referring to ran deeper than she would care to admit.

“That’s fucking rubbish,” Samantha said refusing to give Ruth eye contact.

"I have touched a nerve haven't I Sammy," Ruth said trying to get her to look at her.

"No I am not gay or anything," Samantha said in disgust.

"You don't attack someone for no reason and you said you're not homophobic, so what is it?" Ruth said probing her.

"Fuck you!" Samantha said unable to answer properly.

"I will find out I am not being hated for nothing, you must have a reason, and so what is it," Ruth was determined to find out the truth.

"Okay you're right," she turned and looked at Ruth. "My sister committed suicide because she was a lesbian, her girlfriend and she had a fight and her friend left her. She said it was due to watching you and Pamela on television that convinced her that she was gay. She followed your story and when things went wrong she took her own life."

"I am sorry," Ruth said sincerely.

"No I am sorry, I blamed you but I can see now I was wrong," Samantha admitted.

At that moment the room shook and books started to fly in mid-air. They were both dodging the books and then noticed a snake slither out of the mirror. Ruth pushed Samantha to the floor as a series of poison darts flew in the air and pinned Ruth to the door. Samantha got up and managed to block a dart with a book as it was flying towards Ruth's head, then the snake travelled towards Samantha with its mouth wide open. At that moment Pamela appeared and grabbed the snake and threw it back into the mirror, but only Samantha saw Pamela who smiled at her before she vanished.

The mirrors were becoming more intense as the evil seemed to consume each mirror, it would appear that nothing could stop them. A cycle of murders had inevitably influenced the mirrors or the evil that caused the initial murder possessed all three mirrors. The force was undeniably strong and had the power to control, influence and possess the mind. Pamela appeared and captured John's spirit binding him securely with a rope; he struggled but was unable to break free.

He had little power when Pamela and Annabelle were involved, especially with all their personalities combined; John had become weak and helpless.

Annabelle assisted her in throwing him into a dark room and then the audience assembled in the study to witness the mirrors come to life.

By this time the others came in with the other mirrors, John appeared but was taken away by Pamela and Annabelle who bound him and put him in a dark place. Once the mirrors were up Annabelle's other personalities were freed and the host personality appeared to everyone. Each person sat down and watched as Annabelle appeared in the central mirror. She had strange eyes at first and blood on her neck.

"Thank you for freeing me from the darkness that dwells within these mirrors, my personalities have joined their host, the real me and I are one again. Please don't be alarmed by my head as I will explain it all to you keep watching these mirrors as I convey the story of how I became imprisoned in the mirrors," everyone looked at each other in disbelief, it was like watching a movie of Annabelle's past.

"Here lies the mystery of the mirrors which will astonish and shock you as I tell the tale. The story will unfold and you will be enlightened by your experience although no one will believe where you have heard the story from, I am Annabelle. Although I cannot offer you evidence of this experience I can provide you with reassurance that nothing else will happen to you on your journey of enlightenment".

"Thank God for that!" Elliot said then looked at the others. "Sorry," he said apologetically.

"It all began at here at Harrington Manor I was the Lady of the Manor and I lived with my husband John Harrington who was lord of the manor, we had no children as I had numerous miscarriages probably due to the way I was treated. John was a cruel and jealous man who beat me and locked me away in a dark room, sometimes I was missing for days. I shouted but nobody heard me, I banged at the door and tried turning the handle but it was no use. I could feel things crawling on me and screamed; eventually I was set free from my captivity. John used to humiliate me and mock me in front of the servants, I felt trapped even outside the dark room. John encouraged the maids to flirt with him and even had sex with some of them, usually when I was pregnant or sick of him raping me. I used to go for walks in the woods this was my freedom away from the Manor and his family who considered him perfect. It was during one of my walks in the woods that I met an artist by the name of Ralph Bedford, he was kind and courteous, a true gentleman who treated me nice. He was sat drawing pictures of the trees near a stone bridge, at first I was a little shy and perhaps nervous of him, but then I got used to him. I used to wash my hands and face in the stream that ran under the bridge; Ralph was amused by this and used to gasp at my beauty. He eventually invited me into his cottage and offered me tea and cake just to be treated like this was so nice."

The silence was broke by Samantha who was sobbing to herself, comforted by Elliot.

Annabelle continued with her story her face kept changing in complexion and she was looking like she looked when she met Ralph. Ralph could not take his eyes off me; he told me that he was captivated by my beauty. It was then that he asked me to model for him; I was shy at first as I posed for a portrait and he painted me on canvas. He started with a head and shoulders painting using oils, then as I became more comfortable with him I undressed and posed naked. He was observing my beauty spending hours perfecting all the curves and crevices of my body, just like when he was drawing the trees. At this point we must have fallen in love and made love together for the first time, it was a wonderful experience unlike John; Ralph was gentle and treated me like a lady. Although his hands were rough from his work he was so strong, he treated me as if I were a fragile object or flower. After this day we met regularly and I was so in love, I felt my heart flutter and my whole body tingled in his presence, I believe he felt the same although he was a man of few words. He did announce that he loved me so many times and not just when we made love." Annabelle's voice began to change as she began to speak about the next events, she sounded upset as her voice quivered.

"It was a warm summer's day when I went for my usual walk in the woods, John and I had been arguing, he wanted to try for a baby, but his very presence began to repulse me and I left the house. I was unaware of him following me, he had evidently realised that I was having an affair and wanted to find my lover. I met Ralph in the usual place wearing a hooded top and jeans, Ralph was sat smoking his pipe on a rock by the bridge, drawing the stream and bridge that we liked so much, close by was a wishing well. He warned me to be careful as the well was deep and could be dangerous, I noticed he had brown leather bound book at his side. When I asked him what it was he became defensive as if he was keeping some sort of secret from me. We then went inside the cottage to his studio where I observed some souvenirs from South America and other exotic places. I noticed a sheet covering something large and asked about it, he explained it was some kind of gift for me. Out of curiosity I moved part of the sheet and something pricked my finger, I collapsed and when I awoke I saw a snake coming towards me. It was enormous with a large mouth that was trying to devour me. At that moment Ralph came into my room like a knight in shining armour, the snake simply disappeared and Ralph said that I was imagining things. The only thing under the sheet were the three mirrors that he had made as gifts for me; he had been carving the wooden frames."

Annabelle indicated the blood stains on each frame, "These blood stains belong to Ralph he told me that much, he had tried to clean if off, but he couldn't remove it. He did it on a chisel when carving one of the women's heads, apart from women's heads there were animals that he had seen in jungles and deserts everywhere. I felt better after a glass of water and Ralph's soothing words; I went home and returned the following day. I was followed again by John who by now knew about Ralph and myself. I posed for him naked as usual and this time Ralph and I made love in the studio, little knowing that John was watching from outside. After my visit I walked the usual way home and John entered the studio, he was so quiet Ralph was unaware of his presence. Ralph was relaxing smoking his pipe with his back to the door admiring his painting of me. He grabbed a chisel which was already blood stained from Ralph's accident and plunged it into his back right up to the handle, he then pulled it out and sent it back into his back then thrust the final blow into his neck. He had evidently hit an artery as the blood spurted out everywhere. He then took his pipe that was on the floor and emptied the contents on the floor. He took a match then lit a few flammable objects and started a fire. The studio was burnt to the ground, but amazingly the mirrors remained in tact not even a scorch on them, even the glass was in one piece!"

All Annabelle's audience sat with their mouths open unable to comment at this point, allowing Annabelle to continue her gruesome tale.

"It was then that John planned my disappearance, he had brought the mirrors to the manor and displayed them on the study wall and they were strategically placed as they are now. He had locked me away as usual but before doing told me about Ralph's death and how he knew about our affair. I was so upset that he had not only followed me, but also murdered Ralph in cold blood. I needed to tell someone about everything, but when John set me free he murdered me by stabbing me with that same chisel from the studio and not content with that he got an axe and cut off my head."

Fiona reacted as well as Samantha this time and even Elliot was forced to use his inhaler, each person reacted to the story in some way even Ruth who had witnessed many things.

"He had sent the servants away, saying how upset he was that Annabelle had been unfaithful and had gone missing, he said I had run away in shame. Once he had severed my head from my body he held it up from my hair and boasted to the mirrors. 'See the bitch that dares to fornicate and commit adultery, Ralph behold your lovers head!' With that he put my head in a brown sack and took it to Ralph's well and dropped it down followed by the chisel. As for my body that is buried by the rocks beside the stream you will also find the leather bound book in a hollow part of a tree in a plastic bag. As for John he called back the servants to clean the house, he had always liked Lucy one of the young maids. John committed suicide not by choice I might add, but when he was so remorseful and sad about my death, he was making love to the maid when my head appeared on her shoulders he was so shocked that he threw her to the floor and ran to the window. Lucy lay injured and he threw himself out of the window. That is the full story of my life at Harrington Manor I will now rest in peace knowing that you know the truth."

Annabelle faded away leaving everyone to think about what they had heard and seen, but nobody was able to convey anything to anyone. But at least Annabelle was at rest having told her tale; her spirit was at peace at last. As for the mirrors they suddenly set fire and despite all effort to save them, they disintegrated as they should have done originally in the studio fire. Amazingly nothing else was damaged not even the wall, only the mirrors that had kept the secret hidden inside them.

"Well follow that!" Harrison said completely baffled.

"So tragic," Fiona said, shaking her head in disbelief.

"The poor woman," Ruth said looking at Emma who simply nodded.

"I am really shocked," Samantha said wiping the tears from her eyes.

"What the hell are we going to tell the police about Annabelle's body?" Elliot said confused.

It was finally time for Harrison to leave and take his mirror to Harrington Manor.

ON REFLECTION

Now that the three mirrors were finally together it was thought that they would either consume the Manor or in one mighty wave, cause a massive explosion of energy, or it would endeavour to reveal the secret that has been locked away for so long. Whatever happens has a purpose and the meaning so clear to those seeking the truth. As it happened the truth was revealed and a mystery unravelled no matter how strange it happened.

"So what do we have as evidence that these mirrors even existed and what proof, if any that they were haunted or possessed in some way?" Fiona said leading the discussion.

"Well we all saw Annabelle's image as she relayed a story to us," Emma said confidently. "I also saw Pamela's ghost, now I have not met her before but I described her and Ruth said the description was accurate."

"Thank you Emma, but this would be classed as circumstantial to most people," Fiona said eventually chairing the meeting.

"The pricking of the finger on the corner of each mirror located by the old blood stains," Samantha said pointing to a photograph of the mirror. "I understand that a hole was discovered in this area containing a small cylinder resembling a bullet, inside was a substance that was analysed and found to be some sort of illegal substance that caused not only hallucinations but temporary paralysis."

"Safe to say that a number of people pricked their finger and became exposed to this drug, they then became subjected to all kinds of hallucinations and delusional ideation," Ruth added.

"No doubt the work of James and Margaret Harrington who not only tried to get their hands on the inheritance but also defrauded hotels and many people on the internet with their evil schemes using charity work as their front," Elliot said producing paperwork as evidence.

"I used cameras and bugging devices as further proof of their fraud, I did try to gather evidence of supernatural activity but the sounds were muffled and visibility limited," Harrison said disappointed.

"So what has happened to James Harrington?" Fiona asked.

"He was transferred to a mental health hospital on a secure unit, he was said to be delirious seeing a headless woman and then monkeys around his cell!" Harrison said smiling.

"James was said to have continued to tell his story about his wife being a spider when he killed her and the servant was a snake who he shot in the head and chest," Ruth said looking at Samantha for support.

"Yes Ruth is correct and clearly perceptive with her explanation," Samantha said smiling at Ruth.

"It would also seem that without steering away from the facts that people had a combination of hallucinations and imaginative ideas that were a little confusing. Annabelle herself had a mental illness known as multiple personality syndrome or dissociated personality syndrome which due to past trauma caused her to have an individual personality in each mirror, this needed to be brought back together in order for her to converse with us using the host personality or her real self. Arguably this is a real mental health condition and is very difficult to treat, usually it is done through therapies," Ruth paused looked around then continued. "Coupled with another personality questionably haunting the mirrors who is suggested to be evil may be down to John who evidently influenced James, although I would deem James as a sociopath who has no conscience and will probably spend the rest of his life in psychiatric care," Ruth finally took a breath.

Samantha began clapping encouraging the others to join in; Fiona was astonished by Samantha's sudden change in views and her opinion towards Ruth. Samantha even winked at Elliot which was clearly seen by Fiona who was sat beside her. She leaned and whispered to Elliot hoping Samantha wouldn't see her.

"What on earth did you do to Sammy, and did it involve drugs?" Fiona smiled.

Elliot shrugged his shoulders and he whispered back. "God knows but I hope it lasts!"

"I have something," Chloe shouted and came forward. "I have been to the cottage and discovered a diary tucked inside a tree," she produced a book approximately six inches long by five inches in wide; it had a brown leather cover.

"An entry on the fifth of July 1975 says that he was in the Amazon jungle when he discovered a cave, inside the cave was a series of paintings some seemed to relay a story of a tribe like the Aztecs who had discovered an odd shaped mirror with an image of a woman's head severed from a body, she was said to be some sort of sorceress and slain by warriors for putting a curse on their family," she looked at her audience who seemed to be in a trance. "Shall I go on?"

"Yes Fiona," said curious.

"This is freaky," Samantha said nervously.

"Go on Chloe," Elliot beckoned.

"Well, other entries are similar until I reached the part that mentioned Ralph being bitten by a poisonous snake, he was helped by a tribe of people who related to him how he was delirious and calling for help as he was attacked by wild monkeys and fell into a swamp."

Chloe passed the book to Harrison who examined it.

"I'm amazed at this even in my Army days I have never come across anything like this," he opened a page on a passage about the glass in the mirrors. "I have ordered the glass mirrors from here as the glass is made from minerals in the jungle and I am looking for wood from the trees in the forest," Harrison looked at his colleagues. "So that's what he was up to and he is suggesting the curse is from the jungle, a so called sorcereress."

"Well thank god the mirrors have been destroyed," Elliot said sighing with relief.

"So all those jungle sounds and experiences were from the Amazon jungle?" Samantha asked.

"Yes it appears so Sammy, but then we are dealing with facts and not fiction," Fiona reminded her.

"Of course but you know what we heard and saw it offers an explanation to me," Samantha said glancing at Elliot and back at Fiona.

Elliot smiled. "Yes no doubt about it Sammy is right, we did hear and see a lot."

"Stuart you know we deal in facts for crime reporting, conjecture or fiction has no bearing or credibility in selling our magazines," Fiona said sternly.

"Come on Fi, you know as well as me that sometimes what we see can't be explained even in the best surroundings where we visualise many things, I refer to ghostly places such as castles and haunted houses." Harrison said.

"Thanks for that Daniel" Samantha said, "You really know how to make a girl feel at home."

"Well we have little solid evidence judging by my camera and Stuart's photo's all seem very grainy and even inferred doesn't show much," Harrison said disappointedly. "In fact I have seen better on that television program Most Haunted!"

"Without the over dramatization you mean," Elliot said laughing.

A NEW START

Once everything was over Emma left the Manor and joined Chloe at Ashley Manor. They were happy together and soon forgot the events that took Place at Harrington Manor at least that was what they told each other. But they both had occasional nightmares of past events and could never forget Annabelle's severed head displayed in the mirror. Nobody ever looked at mirrors the same again without thinking that something was going to jump out at them, grabbing or clawing at them in a frenzied attack showing no mercy.

Elliot was driving home with Samantha; he was listening as usual to his classical music which Samantha loved so much.

"Oh come on Stuart this is funeral music," Samantha said rolling her eyes.

"You have no idea, this is quality music," Elliot said.

"Music to sleep through," Samantha said complaining.

"So have a sleep," he advised.

"I don't want to," she replied in an aggravated manner.

"Ok you win, put something on you like," he said keeping the peace.

Samantha looked through her bag and removed a compact disc from its case; she put it in the player. That's what you get by Paramore began to play.

"There we are real music," she said jigging around in her seat.

After they had been driving for a while Elliot was feeling tired, he swerved to miss what he thought was an animal on the road, which made Samantha think of Harrington Hall and Annabelle's tragedy.

"What the fuck was that?" she asked.

"I don't know I couldn't make it out," Elliot said continuing to drive.

"Stop!" Samantha said alarmed.

"Here we go," Elliot said.

"Stop the fucking car now!" Samantha said angrily.

Elliot stopped the car in a layby and got out not knowing what to expect from Samantha.

"I don't believe you Stuart Elliot," Samantha said pacing up and down.

"What do you mean?" Elliot said confused.

"You really don't care do you?" Samantha said flapping her arms about. "That poor creature could be injured and you just don't give a shit."

"What's this really about Sammy?" Elliot said knowing there was something else wrong with her.

"It's you, you're so insensitive at times, not a thought for others and God you annoy me," Samantha was getting tearful again.

"Oh come on that's not fair," Elliot said. "I have helped you and been close to you, now I am insensitive!"

"Yes," she paused. "No, I don't know!" She said confused.

"Indecisive Sammy again," Elliot said trying to get Samantha to say what she truly felt.

"I can't help it Elliot, I mean Stuart, I mean god knows what," she said putting her hands over her face. "I can see Annabelle every time I close my eyes and it's so sad, why couldn't she be happy with Ralph, its not fair, why Stuart?"

"I don't know but you're wearing the grass out beneath your feet" Elliot said trying to make her smile.

"Take us for instance enjoying each other having casual sex, no ties" She said ignoring what he said. "We're happy!"

"Well I am," he said still trying to get a reaction.

"So why couldn't she be happy?" Samantha continued. "What?" she said realising what he said.

"I said I am happy," Elliot waited a moment for her to react.

Inevitably she did react by slapping his face, and then thumping him repeatedly on the chest.

"Elliot!" She shouted in a fit of temper, "I love you."

She then held him and cried uncontrollably, she remained in his arms for a considerable time until they both returned to the car. The radio played 'Strange Magic' by ELO which seemed very appropriate for the occasion regarding the mirrors and how it had brought them together.

CURSED BY AZTECS

In a market in South America a man was selling an assortment of mirrors with hand carved frames similar to Ralph's mirrors. He seemed keen to sell them and explained that they were designed to look like Aztec Tribes, he was quite convincing and foreign tourists did buy them. They were exported around the world and displayed on walls in houses unknowing that these mirrors had the same Aztec Curse that Ralph's had recently. The glass contained a wicked spirit that would cause problems for many people, but no one was aware of this or the sorceress that cursed them.

Back in London, England the criminal reporters and photographers of Criminal World magazine involved with the Harrington Curse story got together in order to discuss the story. As so much had happened and things needed clarifying each person involved needed to sort out fact from fiction. A lot of amazing things had occurred that involved investigation from the team, even from the idea of hallucinations and factual occurrences would have to be discussed in detail before a proper story could be written. Samantha and Elliot were sorting out the story from their perspective while Fiona was clarifying things on the phone with Ruth, Harrison had collected evidence from his sound and camera equipment, he had also had Ralph Bedford's diary and had researched Aztec history.

Fiona sat in as chairwoman in the absence of her father who was playing golf in Scotland with Gordon MacGregor his Scottish friend.

"Ok folks, let's begin this meeting," Fiona said confidently. "Now I realise we discussed this at Harrington Manor, but we really need to get clarification about what we saw and what evidence we have to substantiate our find."

Each of them looked at each other in turn, and then they nodded in agreement.

"So let's begin with you Sammy," Fiona said looking at Samantha.

"Oh yes well" Samantha paused looking at Elliot for support. "We witnessed many things but have little concrete evidence, mostly visions and sound which were said to be hallucinations."

"Yes I agree," Elliot said producing photographs that only showed shadows and blurred images.

"Not much in the way of facts, I am afraid all we have for sure is our own statements."

"Well Daniel, the floor is yours it seems," Fiona said very much in control of the meeting.

Other journalists were present and eager to here what Harrison had to say, they were hoping that he would reveal some amazing facts.

"I realise that we are discussing mainly about the Harrington Curse myth or fact, however I must explain about the origins of these mirrors that most people didn't know about. For instance are you aware of an earlier curse on these mirrors that goes back in history. In around 1511 an Aztec sorceress was killed by the Spanish who had invaded Mexico, she was stabbed and beheaded because the Spanish Army feared her. They then dropped her into the volcano hoping to destroy her powers; instead she became more powerful and put a curse on the Spanish and their descendants through to today. Ralph's diary revealed that he had Spanish blood, but so did John Harrington thus the curse continues today."

"So, what about the jungle sounds and how do you explain them?" Samantha asked.

"Well Ralph used to travel a lot and one of his favourite places was South America and Egypt, although his best known place was Mexico. He studied Aztec history particularly the Tenochtitlan's who were known for their markets visited by countless people supporting their economy. The Aztecs were also highly developed socially, intellectually and artistically,"

Harrison showed a number of pictures on a screen from his laptop.

"This is all fascinating but what about the mirrors?" Samantha asked.

"I am coming to that, bear with me." Harrison said. "The Aztecs worshipped a number of Gods like Huitzilopochtli a God of war and of the sun, the Aztecs made human sacrifices, they practiced divination using the surface of a bowl of water as a mirror. Some mirrors were fashioned from obsidian used by English alchemist John Dee, these mirrors of black obsidian are a type of shiny volcanic glass these played a central role in their mythology and religious rituals of the Aztecs and Mexicana. Tezcatlipoca means smoking mirrors thus the mist seen by James when he murdered his wife Margaret mistaking her for a giant spider. It all gets involved as the mythological story tells about the smoking mirror replacing the foot of a God as he battles against an earth monster But Aztec magicians would divine the future while looking into the obsidian's reflections."

"So what you're saying is that some of the things we experienced with the mirrors go back to the Aztecs and the sorceress head was the same as Annabelle's?" Samantha asked. "Does that also mean that the sorceress cursed the mirrors?"

"I am saying it is a possibility that's all, I have no evidence of this, also the voice could have been talking in the Aztec language and that's why you couldn't understand her. As for the snakes and other creatures you know about, they were to do with the desert and jungles of Mexico and South America I am merely offering suggestions for the hallucinations. The sacrifices made by the Aztecs to their Gods were because they believed that the Gods were nourished by living hearts and that this made the sun rise the next day. Sacrificial ceremonies varied from small to large according to the power of their God. This explains the type of people they were and their obsession for worship. The Spanish Army wanted to destroy the Aztecs and probably feared their beliefs as the Spanish were Catholics and considered witchcraft and sorcery as evil. The sorceress was a threat to them and so they destroyed her by stabbing her to death and then severing her head from her body. They then threw her into the flaming fire in the volcano and destroyed what was left of her. Her spirit was said to have remained and entered the obsidian, thus cursing the mirrors afterwards when they began creating them."

"So the mirrors were cursed?" Elliot asked.

"It appears so if you believe the legend," Fiona replied.

"So she caused all the problems at the Harrington household?" Samantha asked.

"That may be a contributory factor but it all seems a little difficult to believe," Harrison said.

"Well let's get this thing wrapped up and present a story for our readers," Fiona said eager to begin a new story called 'The Harrington Curse.'

Meanwhile in Mexico mirrors are being packaged for export all over the world and in England in one Stately Home a lady is brushing her hair ready to go out when suddenly a thin hand with long sharp nails grabs her by the throat and throttles the life out of her. Her body lies on the floor covered in blood and an image appears in the mirror of the Aztec sorceress!

THE CURSE OF ZYANYA

ORIGINS

In New York a family had recently moved into a new home, Steve and Julie Fierro were very happy designing each room in a classic Spanish style based on Steve's ancestral home back in Spain. But the most exciting feature was the mirror that was exported from Mexico; this resembled a mirror that his Great Uncle had in his home which was also exported from Mexico based on an Aztec design from around 1538.

When the parcel arrived Julie got really excited and tore open the package she revealed a large beautifully decorated mirror based on the obsidian style. This was once considered a 'smoking mirror' going back to the Aztec people who perfected such mirrors back in the 14th century. Julie hung it proudly on her wall in the hall so that everyone entering the house would see it. All was well until night time when the mirror came to life, what followed was a complete nightmare for Steve and Julie.

One stormy night the same day that the mirror arrived Steve and Julie were lying in bed when they heard the sound of breaking glass, Steve went to investigate and discovered mirrors were broken in the lounge and the kitchen. He returned upstairs and walked into the bathroom as he entered the door a great crash occurred and glass shattered and flew into the air, splinters rained onto the floor and buried themselves into Steve's body. He shielded is face with his arms in order to protect his eyes, but his feet were torn to ribbons as exited the bathroom.

Meanwhile Julie was experiencing another phenomenon, a snake was moving towards her slithering across the floor. She screamed falling back onto the bed scared and confused, she saw Steve's ancient Japanese sword on the wall so she pulled it down and began swinging it in the air. She heard Steve's voice as he shouted to her, but insisted on destroying the snake first. With a few blows of the sword she was satisfied that the snake was dead; she heard every slash and blow as the sword contacted the body. Unfortunately after she calmed down she discovered her husband's body on the floor he was covered in blood. By the time the police arrived Julie was in shock and still holding the sword. Steve was lying dead slashed to death with a sword; there was no sign of a snake but a lot of broken glass all over the house. It was thought by the police that Julie had broken all the mirrors in a frenzied attack around the house and finally killed her husband. She was arrested and jailed pending trial, eventually she was sent to a mental hospital where she was going to stay for a long time.

AZTEC EMPIRE

The Aztec empire during the sixteenth century was considered the most powerful in Mesoamerica history (Mexican history) of all time with the capital city at Tenochtitlan in the valley of Mexico. This was classed as the heartland of the Aztec civilization, a large internally drained basin surrounded by volcanic mountains. The land is so picturesque with all its colour and rolling hills and the Aztecs even more colourful dressed in white with a multitude of coloured garments and feathers. The people were classed as fine nation goods traders, but they built pyramids and temples for their gods and sacrificed thousands of people mainly slaves.

They had many gods that they worshipped based on the elements of the earth, or the sun or such. This led to their down fall as the Spanish who were Catholics believed them to be pagan worshippers and killed many of the Aztec races, including priests and sorcerers alike.

It was at this time that Zyanya a beautiful woman became involved in sorcery, she convinced a nation of Aztecs that the Gods were happy with her having nursed people to health and demonstrating that her magic could heal many who had fallen down by illness or wounded in battle. She became powerful almost like a goddess. Then the Spanish settled in Mexico and knew of her but it wasn't until a wounded soldier called Domingo Fierro fell in love with her that problems occurred.

Zyanya kissed Fierro tenderly on the lips and began to remove her garments, he tried to speak but she pressed her finger on his mouth.

"Please don't speak enjoy these moments that we have together, for soon you will be joining your friends and you will forget me." Zyanya said tearfully.

"I would never forget you; I love you and want to be with you forever." Fierro said allowing her to caress his body and massage his chest.

"If only it was you and me, we would be free to love each other." Zyanya said stroking his thick black hair.

"Why do we need to tell anyone, we could just run away somewhere?" Fierro said trying to plan things out in his mind.

"No I can't leave my people while the Spanish are here, they are in danger." Zyanya said concerned.

"I understand Zyanya and I will try to help them." Fierro said confidently.

But as they made love they concentrated on the present and everything else hardly mattered, Fierro had been in the cave for months and may have been forgotten. However Zyanya had ventured out of the cave in order to visit her people, she had returned with food and fresh potions to help cure her wounded man. They were happy together until one day someone discovered their secret, she was also fond of Fierro.

A Spanish girl called Andora Martinez was jealous and ran to the captain for advice, Gonzalo Alvarado was furious that one of his crew members had fallen in love with a witch and ordered them to attend his quarters on the ship. They were brought to the captain by the crew of the ship who had been led to the cave by Andora who had been spying on them for a while.

He spoke to Domingo first. "I am disappointed in you Domingo consorting with a heathen, you were brought up a Catholic and know the dangers of getting involved with a witch."

"But Sir she is adorable, a real lady highly respected amongst her race, she saved my life." Fierro said in her defence.

"I don't care we are going to make an example of this witch and tread on these native heathens." Alvarado said angrily.

"I suppose Andora has told you of our love, she is evidently jealous. You know that." Fierro asked. "What are you going to do?"

"Flog and behead her in front of her people and then I am going to crush their religion by killing the priests and other religious heathens."

"No!" Fierro shouted.

"Yes!" Alvarado shouted back then addressed the guards "Take him away and put him in irons."

"You're making a mistake Captain please stop before it's too late!" Fierro said as he was escorted out.

"Bring the woman to me." Alvarado ordered

Zyanya stood before Alvarado dressed in her Aztec finery with her head dress and colourful clothing; she looked beautiful and seemed to show no fear. She stared into the eyes of Alvarado and examined her enemy appearing to see beyond his evil eyes.

She then spoke in her native language which translated seemed like a curse not only directed to the Captain but anyone averse to the Aztec race.

"Curses on you and your people for your evil work said to be part of your religion and culture. I curse anyone who is opposed to my people, and our beliefs; I curse you and your descendants. May anyone who possesses the treasures of my people including the smoking mirrors be cursed too and die horrible deaths!" Zyanya said in her native tongue.

"You have caused disruption and revolt against my people, I will therefore set an example of you by having you flogged and humiliated before your people, and then I will have you beheaded in a public place." Alvarado said angrily.

The Captain became fearful and nervous seeing her eyes staring at him, he ordered the guards to take her away until the time of her execution.

By late afternoon the crowds had gathered in front of the temple and before their eyes Zyanya was flogged and executed as the Captain had ordered. Not satisfied with this he ordered the execution of some of the priests and other popular Aztec leaders, he wasn't happy until 3,000 people were killed on that day. It was one of the bloodiest days in Spanish history but more bloodshed occurred before the Captain decided to set sail back to Spain. As he sat in his cabin all he could see was the eyes of Zyanya staring at him both when he condemned her to death and at her execution. Even when he held up her severed head by her hair to show her people, he saw those eyes and dropped her head to the ground. It was as if she had already begun her curse on him. Lying in the corner of the room was one of the smoking mirrors which began to illuminate filling the room with light. Alvarado covered his eyes from the immense light but heard a voice, loud and clear in his own language.

"Cursed are you Alvarado. May you and your family burn in hell forever!"

He uncovered his eyes to see the severed head of Zyanya hovering in mid air her eyes were burning and her tongue had turned into the shape of a snake. She spit at him and his body was engulfed in flames. Estaban the cabin boy witnessed the event and reported back to Fierro who was in chains below deck. Andora was running around on the deck of the ship her face was petrified, suddenly a rope wrapped itself around her neck and she was pulled up reaching the mast and there she swung strangled to death. A fire began near some cannons, gunpowder exploded and the ship caught fire, the crew ran frantically from one place to another, trying to escape. Eventually all the crew perished all but Estaban and Fierro who narrowly escaped in a small boat, Estaban saved the life of Fierro and they made their way back to Mexico. The Captain had died from spontaneous human combustion as there was no evidence of fire around the cabin only the captain had set alight!

Prior to her death Zyanya and others created a number of mirrors these were sold in a local market. Later in the twenty first century the mirrors were copied using material from the same volcano and sold in the same market. They too were exported around the world, but what people failed to realise was that these too were cursed by the witch due to the fact they were from the same volcano. Zyanya had cursed the volcano and all around it in order to protect her culture - the Aztec people; anyone taking anything from the volcano was destined to receive a horrible death. Like the fate of Steve and Julie in New York, Steve died but Julie existed in a living hell with the memory of her husband's death looming over her head.

Back at criminal world magazine in London, the team were discussing this strange phenomenon

"Daniel I need to speak to you." Fiona said seriously.

"Am I in trouble?" Harrison asked concerned.

"You are one of my finest reporters, why would you be in trouble?"

"But you sound so serious is it one of those cases that we go to and find that we are part of the mystery or crime?" Harrison asked inquisitively.

"Dan we do that all the time so nothing is different there!" Fiona said slightly amused by his reaction.

"We've been mixed up with some shady characters of late." Harrison admitted.

"Do you remember the Harrington curse?" Fiona asked.

"Yes, how can I forget the cursed mirrors and all they entailed?" Dan replied. "Tell me it isn't that?"

"I'd like to say no, but I have had some disturbing phone calls about mirrors from our readers, some may be a hoax. However some people seemed to tell convincing stories about mirrors and events that take place similar to our own." Fiona seemed anxious.

"I thought you and I could travel to one place while Sammy and Stuart could visit another place." Fiona was working through papers on her desk.

"I take it their relationship is still good?" Harrison said amused.

"You know them they blow hot and cold, Sammy is Sammy bless her."

"Listen, I need you to go to New York to interview a woman called Julie Fierro who allegedly killed her husband." Fiona explained.

"I see and why allegedly?" Harrison asked inquisitively.

"Mirrors were involved." Fiona said hoping he would respond.

"Oh I see cursed mirrors no doubt?" Harrison said realising what she was referring to.

"Take Samantha if you wish." Fiona offered.

"I would rather take you to be honest Fiona." Harrison said considering the situation.

"I can understand Sammy can be a little inconsiderate and abrupt maybe." Fiona admitted.

"So you will come with me?" Harrison asked.

"Yes I'll send Sammy and Stuart to Spain where a similar thing occurred. Get packed and I'll phone you later."

"Right I'll get prepared." Harrison agreed.

At that point Samantha entered the room; she was as elegant as ever spoilt only by her foul tongue or sewer mouth as some people called her.

"Hi Sammy." Both Fiona and Harrison greeted her.

"What's going on?" Samantha asked knowing that she had interrupted something.

"Oh we were discussing the New York incident." Harrison explained.

"Yes a terrible tragedy." Fiona said.

"I know I read that she chopped her husband up with his own Japanese sword!" Samantha said sitting behind her desk.

"We're going to investigate the crime." Fiona explained.

"You and Dan are going to New York?" Samantha asked.

"Yes while you and Stuart go to Spain." Fiona said smiling.

"Well as long as it isn't fucking spooky castles or cursed mirrors!" Samantha said frowning.

"Sammy for god sake what's the matter with you?" Fiona asked.

"What's the matter, we've faced some things, followed up some storylines but I hate creepy castles and houses and what we witnessed with the mirrors. Tell me it's not one of those is it?" Samantha said nervously.

"I am afraid to say it is." Fiona said reluctantly.

"I fucking knew it, which one?" Samantha asked not really wanting the answer to her question.

"Those cursed mirrors." Harrison said leaving the room.

"But we lifted the curse when we put them together didn't we?" Samantha looked pale.

"Apparently not as they go back much further in history to Aztec times, the origin is in Mexico. The mirrors were made from the minerals found in a volcano where a witch called Zyanya once lived in a nearby cave." Fiona showed Samantha some paperwork on the subject.

"So what are we doing?" Samantha asked.

"Finding out where the mirrors are and the damage they have caused, and then somehow we need to return them all to their origin." Fiona explained.

"So how did they get to other countries?" Samantha asked reading the details.

"Exported by tourists going to a market in Mexico, they are all over the world probably causing havoc." Fiona showed

Samantha addresses of some people who had mirrors in their possession.

"So many people affected it could take months!" Samantha said.

"Yes it could well do but do you remember the damage those other three mirrors caused until we got them together?" Fiona said pointing out the work ahead.

"Yes I remember it well." Samantha said thinking back to some of the incidents.

"I'm thinking about taking Ruth Ashley the mental health nurse to help me talk to Julie, she is more experienced in this area." Fiona said waiting for a homophobic reaction from Samantha.

"Good idea she will probably have some answers." Samantha replied taking Fiona by surprise.

"Well you do surprise me Sammy no homophobic reaction?" Fiona looked her in the eyes still trying to get a reaction.

"Honestly Fi I thought you knew about that." Samantha was staring back at her. "Ruth and I had a bit of a disagreement and I explained about my sister committing suicide because she was not accepted as a lesbian in society, I blamed people like Ruth and Pamela for publicly flaunting their affair. Ruth explained the facts about modelling and about her ex psycho pursuing them and Pamela getting killed as a result of that maniac. It all made sense and at the end of the day society is to blame for homophobia, that includes religion and politics they all fuck your life up in the end!". Samantha was getting upset and angry at the same time.

"I did notice how well you were getting on with Ruth at the Harrington household, you amaze me sometimes." Fiona admitted.

"Oh Fi, I am reasonable sometimes I just get so fucked off with some people,

so I let them know it, I can't help being outspoken and opinionated."

Samantha explained.

IN SEARCH OF MIRRORS

Fiona, Ruth and Harrison headed to New York. On the plane they compared notes and discussed just how they were going to question Julie Fierro about her husband and the events that took place in New York. Ruth was aware that the American mental health system may be different to England and that they had to be discrete about the mirrors. She could be accused of reinforcing Julies delusions regarding what she actually saw, which would not help her on her road to recovery. But at the same time she needed to know the facts in order for them to deal with the mystery behind the mirrors.

Ruth explained to the staff that they were there to cover the story and try to help in some way.

They arrived at Julie's house and were introduced to Julie's older sister Amy and her husband Jim by a cousin Gillian, Amy introduced her daughters Jackie aged twenty six and

Patricia or Pepper as everyone called her due to her odd taste in food, she was eighteen. Amy was forty years old and big boned; she was quite over weight with a lot to say finding every opportunity to speak badly about Julie in her absence.

"I don't care what anyone says she killed poor Jim for no reason and in a horrific way!" Gillian said shaking her finger at her audience.

Pepper stood up and shouted back at Amy. "Julie would never willingly harm anyone even you for your vicious tongue!" Pepper was a blonde haired very slim and normally a quiet lady.

"She's right. Pepper you tell her." Jackie agreed.

"Now girls Gillian is merely expressing her opinion on what is obviously a tragic situation, let's calm down and have something to eat."

Nothing else was said that evening; everyone retired to bed and all was quiet that night, everyone slept soundly and they all met in the dining room the next morning for breakfast, before going to visit Julie at the hospital.

Julie was sat in a room it was quite empty with a table and a half a dozen chairs neatly placed around the table, across the room was a mirror which also served as a window on the other side where staff could observe the interview.

Ruth introduced herself and Fiona and explained about the magazine Criminal World and how they would present the facts to the public. The object was to help her come to terms with her loss and get her back into society. Julie agreed to the interview as long as they recorded the facts and stated it was her fault; she didn't really want to return to society as she felt that she was a danger to the public.

"Julie I know you have told this story many time and relived it in your mind, but tell us what happened that night." Ruth asked

"We heard strange noises like wild life, strange like jungle sounds, then breaking glass, Steve my husband went to investigate that was the last time I saw him alive." Julie became tearful.

"Go on Julie you're doing fine." Ruth encouraged her to continue.

"I heard Steve coming back up the stairs and he entered the bathroom, I heard more breaking glass and wanted to find out what was happening I could hear him yelling it must have been the splinters of glass hitting him and piercing his body. I went to leave the room when an enormous snake came straight towards me; I fell off the bed and stood with my back to the wall hoping Steve would return."

"Then what happened?" Fiona asked.

"He didn't come and so I remembered the Japanese sword on the wall, I reached up just in time for the snake to contact my body. I pulled the sword from its cover and started striking the snake, I could tell when I hit the snake because it made a thud then I repeatedly hit the snake cutting of parts of it at a time until there was no movement. I closed my eyes for a moment or at least it seemed like a moment, when I opened them it was daylight and my husband was lying across the bed hacked to pieces. I killed him; there was blood everywhere on the bed, splashed on the floor and walls. Gillian came in she contacted the ambulance crew and phoned the police, I was told that they found me in shock staring at my husband's body."

"It's okay Julie; everything is going to be fine." Ruth said reassuringly.

"You actually believe me don't you?" Julie asked.

"Of course we do." Fiona said smiling.

"So where did the mirror come from?" Ruth asked.

"It was from Mexico, my husband liked it because it reminded him of the Aztecs and his Spanish ancestors who travelled to Mexico in 1538, and they taught the Aztecs about Spanish culture and Catholicism. The Roman Catholic religion was brought to ancient Mexico by the Spanish. I have heard since this time that the Spanish empire was as cruel as the British Empire of its day. Are the mirrors cursed? Is it them that caused me to do what I did at the time? If so I may be redeemed." Julie pleaded.

"We can't say there is too much speculation, but we believe the mirrors hold the key to what is happening in many places." Ruth said looking at the mirror behind them.

"So there are more of them? How many more?" Julie asked gripping Ruth's arm her nails began to dig into Ruth's flesh and she began to bleed.

Ruth pulled her hand off and held her wound tightly; the blood trickled through her fingers.

"I'm sorry please forgive me." Julie said looking at some of the blood on her hands.

Julie began to scream thinking back to when she was with Steve, holding the sword and the blood dripping from it onto her night dress. She continued to scream until the medical team came in and held onto her. One of the nurses sedated her using an injection and she soon settled down.

"What on earth were you doing?" One nurse asked.

"Facing her with her fears and providing reassurance." Ruth replied

"You have set her back in her treatment and re-enforced her delusions." The nurse insisted.

"You have no idea what has happened to this woman have you!?" Ruth shouted.

"She was experiencing visual hallucinations, I know that and you told her it was all real, she has a mental illness but as yet we don't know what." The nurse continued. "A type of neurosis, maybe schizophrenia."

“You base that on one episode of query hallucinations, no other history and I presume nothing since that time, what kind of fucking diagnosis is that?” Ruth replied angrily.

“I demand that you leave this hospital at once before I call security.” The nurse insisted.

“Come on Ruth we’ve out stayed our welcome let’s go.” Fiona encouraged Ruth to leave guiding her with her hand on shoulder.

Meanwhile back at the household Harrison was being entertained by Julie’s relatives, Harrison was sat reading a book in the study. Fiona and Ruth went out for lunch in order to have a quiet discussion about Julie and their harrowing interview.

Harrison was called for lunch, everyone was eating in the kitchen, and Amy was making pancakes and burgers as an easy option as they would be having a cooked evening meal. Pepper had her usual odd mix of marmalade on her pancakes and pepper on a burger, while the others had maple syrup on pancakes and ketchup on their burgers. All seemed calm until Gillian entered the room and began a discussion on Julie; she sat and addressed her audience who dreaded her entering the room.

“So I wonder what amazing excuse Julie has come up with this time with your friends?” Gillian said looking at Harrison.

"I 'm sure they will return with some answers," Harrison replied trying to avoid eye contact with her.

At that moment her plate was suddenly swarming with ants, the whole plate was black, everyone looked on in disbelief as only her plate was affected. Then it spun around and flew off the table and broke against the wall, this was followed by the clock falling from the wall. The time showed clearly on the face as ten o'clock in the morning when in reality it was midday. Harrison looked at his watch which indicated the right time; Amy did the same and looked at Harrison.

"What time was Julie's interview?" Amy asked.

"10.00 am!" Harrison replied.

"Oh come on Amy you don't think this was some sort of weird event someone set all this up as a prank!" Gillian said.

"Like who?" Amy asked.

"Well any one of you. Probably Pepper trying to make Julie look innocent!" Gillian said pointing her finger at Pepper.

"How dare you accuse me of such childish pranks, tell me how could I cover your plate with ants!" Pepper said in her own defence.

"Yes Gillian and where are the ants now?" Jackie said defending her sister.

Jackie walked toward the broken plate and pointed to the floor, as she had said there was no evidence of ants. Not one dead body and what was even more unusual the clock face had changed back to twelve o'clock midday.

"I still think its some kind of trick; you can't fool me - any of you." Gillian said sharply.

"Gillian if you think my girls would stoop as low as to do this, well you're a fool!" Amy said in disgust.

"I will get to the bottom of this believe me and you will see that your girls are no angels." Gillian said leaving the room.

Amy looked at her girls although she didn't say anything to Gillian she was wondering whether or not Gillian was right in what she said.

"I'd better not find out that you two have been tricking your cousin." Amy said clearing away the dishes.

"Mother really we didn't do anything she is totally wrong." Pepper said echoed by Jackie who was picking up the fragments of plate.

"I have seen a lot of strange events recently and I can tell you many stories regarding strange phenomenon, but I don't want you to begin to believe that you have seen things by putting ideas into your head. But put it this way we are not just investigating Julie, we believe there is more to Julie's experience than you know about. Only you can experience things and see for yourself what is real and what is not, find the facts out for yourself." Harrison explained.

"What are you talking about? The supernatural?" Jim asked.

“If you want to put it like that then, yes the supernatural.” Harrison replied.

“That’s insane everything can be explained!” Jim said dismissing Harrison’s theory.

“So you mean ghosts?” Pepper asked.

“Sort of!” Harrison replied reluctant to discuss the subject further

“This is crazy you don’t expect us to swallow all this?” Jim continued. “Gillian is right someone is playing a prank.”

“I’ll reserve judgement until we get more answers.” Harrison said leaving the room.

Fiona and Ruth arrived after the event and updated Harrison about Julie. There were no further developments to support the activities of the mirror or its curse.

Later that evening Gillian was lying on her bed when she heard strange sounds in the room, it was as if she was in a jungle with wild creatures. She looked around staring into the darkness and trying make out the shapes moving around the room. She felt for a torch that she kept on a cupboard near her bedside on the left hand side, eventually she found it and felt for the switch on the side of the torch. Switching it on she then shone the narrow beam around the room, shouting at the same time.

“Pepper if that’s you messing around!” She shouted.

Nothing was seen and so she slid her legs out of the bed, as she did so she felt something grab both legs, it was wet and slimy with sharp claws. She felt as if she was being pulled into a swamp her legs were disappearing into something wet. She let out a scream as she was being sucked down she was almost fully submerged when the door burst open and Amy rushed in. Amy switched on the light to find Gillian lying on the floor; she was wrapped in her bed sheet and staring into space.

"Gillian what's wrong are you hurt?" Amy asked.

"No I'm fine." Gillian said annoyed with her display of screaming.

Everyone else entered the room all surprised to see Gillian on the floor wrapped in her bedding.

"Go ahead all stare at me and have a good laugh!" Gillian said angrily.

"No one is laughing at you, did you have a nightmare?" Jim asked.

"No I damn well didn't, it was probably your girls again playing pranks!" Gillian said getting herself up with help from Amy and Jim.

"I felt like I was in a swamp and something grabbed me and was pulling me down I was wet and scared." Gillian admitted.

"Wait a minute, if you were wet and in a dirty swamp why are you clean and dry now?" Fiona asked.

"Ask Pepper she will know." Gillian said pointing at the tired looking girl who was shaking her head.

"Not me I was asleep, ask Jackie." Pepper said looking at Jackie for support.

Jackie nodded in agreement and then looked around the room; she could also see that nothing had been disturbed.

"Let's all go back to bed." Jim said.

Later that night Pepper heard something in her room, she was asleep next to Jackie when suddenly she was lifted off the bed and tossed across the room. Then Jackie was lifted up and suspended in mid air, she was tied with bind weed which tightened around her arms and feet. Pepper saw the weed as it wrapped itself around Jackie's throat and became tighter and tighter. Both Jackie and Pepper were screaming Pepper tried to move forward but was also being tied down by bind weed.

Everyone entered the room and Jackie fell back on the bed, while Pepper collapsed on the floor, Amy ran to Jackie while Jim ran to Pepper.

"Do you still think it's our girls?" Jim asked Gillian.

"No I think it's our guests, they're playing pranks to prove Julie's innocence." Gillian said pointing at Harrison.

“Ask them what they saw.” Ruth said. “Go on ask them!”

“Jackie what did you see?” Amy asked.

“I was lifted in the air and some sort of thick plant wrapped itself around me like a snake its coils tightening and choking me, it gripped my body stopping the blood flow to my arms and legs!” Jackie explained.

“Pepper what did you see?” Her father asked.

“I was lifted up and thrown across the room then I was attacked the same as Jackie, it was real believe me!” Pepper said shaking.

“So do you see bind weed or can you imagine someone holding Jackie up like that or throwing Pepper right across the room?” Ruth asked.

“He could!” Gillian said pointing at Harrison. “He looks strong and capable of anything.”

“I can’t tell you what to believe but I suggest that you look further than this room for the answers to these events, I heard about the ants and the clock and believe me, it’s not us.” Fiona said

“We all want answers for our own reasons, but accusing each other doesn’t help.” Ruth added.

“You know something about what’s going on, what is it?” Jim asked.

"You simply wouldn't believe us." Harrison said.

"Oh you mean about the supernatural?" Jim asked inquisitively.

"I am speaking about being sceptical as I once was, we all question the unknown and seek answers to do with what we can't see or understand. Looking for rational explanations that dismiss the idea of ghosts or other phenomenon's." Harrison tried to explain to a captive audience.

"People have been known to mass hallucinate or think they hear voices, and yes, something's can be explained away by a mental condition or trauma. But some things are not explained - like the swamp that Gillian professes to be in or the bind weed that is no where to be seen. Yes these girls have marks on their arms and feet which cannot be explained or the fact that Jackie couldn't breathe because she was being strangled by this weed. You all need to wise up and stop blaming each other for this." Ruth said looking at Gillian.

"We could leave now and you will find that it isn't us at all, you need to decide if you want our help or not." Fiona said leaving the family with an ultimatum.

"So do you know the answer?" Jim asked.

"Yes we do." Harrison said. "But you really won't believe what you hear!"

"Really!" Gillian said sarcastically. "Do enlighten us!"

"You know the mirror in the hall?" Harrison asked.

"You mean the only one in the house?" Amy asked.

"Yes it's from Mexico it goes back to Aztec times and it is said to be cursed." Harrison explained.

"How do you know?" Gillian asked.

"We have come across these mirrors before and wrote about them in our magazine Criminal World." Fiona said. "But there again why would you!"

"Oh so now you set up a mirror to perform tricks and...." Gillian was

interrupted. "And no I don't read such garbage!"

"For god sake Gillian are you completely fucking stupid, why would we do anything to trick or prank you?" Ruth said angrily.

"I don't know." Gillian said then went silent.

"The answer is you really don't know because you speak crap and are too much of a snob to read good journalism such as Criminal World. The fact is it's too educational for the likes of you!" Ruth replied angrily.

"You must be the one rudest people I have ever met." Gillian said surprised by someone who had actually challenged her.

"All I can say is that you don't meet many people then!" Ruth instantly replied.

"Well I haven't come here to be insulted." Gillian said turning her back on Ruth.

"Well, where do you usually go?" Ruth said feeling her arm being pulled by Fiona.

"Leave it Ruth she really isn't worth it." Fiona advised.

Harrison patted Ruth on the shoulder. "Well done Ruth."

Soon afterwards everyone returned to bed, the next morning people began appearing in the dining room for breakfast. All through the day Fiona and Harrison were contacting people about the other mirrors, while the rest of the family were discussing previous events trying to find answers apart from the mirror being cursed. That evening Gillian had been drinking heavily and dismissing each theory that came to mind. Then Harrison was thrown across the dining room straight past Gillian hitting his head on the wall. He was dazed and confused holding his head and then looking at his hand, he was bleeding not badly but enough to cause him concern. Gillian left the room after telling Amy that she thought it was nonsense about the cursed mirrors and she would prove it. She staggered into the hallway followed by Harrison who was still dazed; Amy was behind him holding a damp tea towel for his head. He took it off her and held it to his head, Pepper and Fiona were coming down the stairs having heard all the noise, Amy noticed Pepper and stopped in her tracks.

"Pepper stay where you are!" Amy said with her hands up.

Gillian appeared in front of the mirror and began to look into it and taunting the image in a playful manner.

"Come on mirror show me what your made of let me see you perform, mirror mirror on the wall who is afraid of you!" Gillian went on.

"Gillian, stop it!" Pepper shouted. "Come away from it!"

"Gillian listen too Pepper, it's dangerous!" Fiona shouted.

"Dangerous it isn't at all, see harmless!" Gillian shouted.

"Get her away from that mirror!" Harrison shouted holding his forehead.

"I see something it's a severed head being held up by her hair; she has fire in her eyes." Suddenly a ball of fire came out of the mirror and hit her in the eyes this was followed by a clawed hand which grabbed her by the throat. Before she had chance to scream the claw tightened and the nails buried themselves into her flesh, blood oozed out and the claw ripped a handful of flesh from her throat. She fell to the ground. The blood was spurting out of her severed arteries. Pepper and Harrison were close enough to get sprayed with blood and both watched in horror as Gillian died.

"Come away Pepper, walk back slowly." Fiona shouted but Pepper stood still and pale and staring at Gillian's lifeless body.

"Pepper take hold of my hand." Harrison put his hand out. "It's okay just take hold of my hand."

At that moment the claw grabbed Harrison's arm and he was forced to look into the mirror, he noticed the face and watched as the eyes changed from fire to sparkling brown eyes. The claw retracted and disappeared back into the mirror, Harrison grabbed Peppers arm and led her away from the mirror and towards Fiona.

"I don't understand you were set free?" Fiona said relieved.

"Yes quite frankly I am amazed too, she could have killed me!" Harrison said sighing with relief.

Samantha and Elliot had arrived in Spain initially at a hotel in Madrid. Samantha gave her usual performance of acting as the innocent party when it came to romance. Elliot was seen to be the predator eager for sex and considered to have no feelings or as Samantha put it thinking with his 'dick'. Their romantic interludes were always entertaining to others as Samantha always seemed to be flirting with Elliot. It was like a hunting game she was the hunter and he was the prey, Samantha the seducer and Elliot the seduced who would submit to her forceful desires. In reality she tried to conceal her true feelings for fear of getting hurt, she really wanted marriage with all the strings and bows. Elliot remained confused by all her emotions and her hormonal rushes that affected her mood, he just considered her unstable and foul mouthed at times. But Samantha was also beautiful and had that coy look that had the ability to melt him like a block of ice. He was kind and sensitive two areas that were considered weak in a woman's eyes. The combination was endearing from a shy and sweet innocent Samantha to a sensitive guy combined with the hormones spelt out dynamite, as Elliot only had to light the fuse and they had an explosive relationship. They stayed one night at the hotel enjoying each others company before going to the Spanish home of Alvarado, set beneath the hills and desert regions of Spain.

They arrived at a Spanish home enjoying the hospitality that Spain had to offer bearing in mind they had an assignment to do searching for Aztec mirrors. Initially they were introduced to the family and servants of the home. A man with a limp approached them he was slim and dark with a large moustache, he introduced himself as Carlos Alvarado head of the household, in turn he introduced his wife Margarita (or Margo) then there was Olivia aged seven and Thomas aged nine. The main servants were Marie the head maid, Stephan the driver and Nikki a young maid, each shook hands with Samantha and Elliot. Margo was in a wheelchair, she had been in a riding accident, and her horse had been startled and threw her out of the saddle. They were shown around the house by Nikki, who seemed reluctant to enter the study where the mirror was hanging on a wooden panelled wall. They reached the bedroom and Nikki stopped by one of the doors, she looked at them with a puzzled expression.

"Are you two together as a couple?" She asked.

"Yes." replied Elliot without hesitation.

"Sort of I suppose." replied Samantha who was reluctant to commit herself.

"Well I will arrange two rooms in case!" Nikki said smiling.

Samantha looked at Elliot without saying a word and then looked back at Nikki. "We need to freshen up, you know, take a shower!"

"Of course, we have dinner in an hour downstairs, informal dress in the dining room." Nikki said opening two doors one for Samantha and the other for Elliot.

They waited for Nikki to leave them before discussing their sleeping arrangements.

"Elliot I'm sorry but I still feel odd about us, you know the love thing!" Samantha tried to explain but felt very awkward with him.

"Sammy don't mention it," he replied.

"Really!" She said confused.

"Yes, don't mention it; I'll see you in an hour." Elliot was obviously upset and his reply was meant to be sarcastic.

Samantha just shrugged her shoulders and entered her room unperturbed by his response; she merely went inside and shut the door behind her.

An hour later Samantha knocked on his door, she wore a dark blue dress and matching shoes, her hair was piled up on top of her head. Elliot wore a white shirt and grey trousers. They headed downstairs and looked for the dining room one of them saw a servant enter a room with food and they followed her.

Carlos was sat at the head of the table he had reserved a seat on either side of him for them.

"Come sit here." He instructed. "We have much to discuss."

"Thank you." Samantha said sitting down and watching Elliot sit opposite.

Samantha had been thinking of what Elliot said and tried to interpret it in different ways, she had had an hour to think about it when she was getting ready. She realised that she had reached Elliot's sensitive area, she felt bad as she knew he really loved her and she was afraid to commit to their relationship.

Elliot was looking at her and admiring how good she looked in her blue dress which seemed to suit her complexion and sparkling eyes. She smiled at him in a way that begged his forgiveness, a sweet and innocent smile that told him she really loved him. He picked up the message and smiled back, and then he looked at Carlos attentively.

"So Carlos what can you tell us about your family?" Elliot asked.

"Yes, we understand there has been tragedy throughout history, stemming from a curse by a witch called Zyanya?"

"It happened centuries ago with my ancestor Captain Gonzalo Alvarado, he was the captain of a ship, a powerful leader who took a number of men to Mexico and befriended the Aztec people. They traded and we shared many things including clothes, vessels and mirrors, they had fine markets. All went wrong when they revolted against Gonzalo because he wanted to put an end to human sacrifices and introduce Christianity to their lives. The witch Zyanya put a love spell on one of the crew Domingo Fierro and caused him to rebel against his ship mates. She was executed demonstrating the fact that the Spanish would not tolerate rebellion and Fierro was put in irons. But before the witch was executed she cursed the Spanish and told them that all would die horrible deaths including the descendants of Gonzalo. This has been so. We have had so much tragedy in the family, some family members have died horrifically. It has been so bad that some family members failed to recognise their own kin, some burnt to death, and some have had their flesh torn from them".

As he was saying this Samantha was cutting the skin from the chicken on her plate and paused with a look of disgust on her face.

"Charming!" She said with the colour draining from her face.

"We think the curse is coming from mirrors which were made from volcanic lava in Mexico." Elliot said awaiting a reaction, he was aware that Carlos version on the Zyanya story was a little different to what he had previously heard and suited the Spanish history better than the Mexican version.

At that point Nikki who was serving food dropped a dish, she was frozen on the spot and staring into space. Marie escorted her out of the room while another servant cleaned the mess off the stone floor.

"Tell me more." Carlos insisted.

"Well, we have been investigating this strange phenomenon, by we I refer to the reporters from Criminal World magazine and the other specialists. We have seen many strange things linked to these mirrors."

"I believe that you have one in the library Carlos?" Samantha asked.

"Yes we do." Carlos replied looking at Margo.

"Yes I had one sent over from Mexico." Margo said.

"But you don't seriously think that a mirror could be causing so many problems?" Carlos said dismissively.

"We can only speculate and explain what we have experienced." Samantha said.

"So that's why you asked about the mirrors." Margo said.

"Have you ever witnessed any activity with the mirrors?"

"The servants have reported seeing a severed head and serpents appearing and slithering out of the mirror. But I have never known anything." Carlos said.

"Your father died in the study he was said to have been petrified by something." Margo said.

"He was mad and experienced a heart attack and died." Carlos said.

"What about that man who set alight before your eyes?" Margo said upset by his reaction.

"Spontaneous human combustion?" Elliot said excitedly.

"So is that strange or coincidental that we are here to investigate these things?" Samantha said. "Glass shattering and forming into clouds of smoke, or strange creatures coming from the mirror?"

"And how do you propose to stop it?" Carlos asked.

"By returning it back to its origin in Mexico." Elliot said.

Samantha had moved around to where Elliot was sitting and placed her finger on his lips. "I think we need to talk Stuart, I propose we discuss things with our colleagues first."

It was late evening when Elliot was lying in bed thinking about the mirrors, he heard the bedroom door creaking open and noticed a figure creeping towards his bed. Only when he felt the warmth of human flesh did he realise that Samantha had entered his bed, she had removed her pyjamas and lay naked beside him. It was obvious what her intentions were as she cuddled up to him and began to massage his bottom with her long thin fingers. Then proceeded to kiss his neck her hot breath travelling to his right ear, he felt her tender lips kissing him passionately and then felt her wet tongue licking him, moving around like a snake. Elliot was getting excited as Samantha noticed his breathing and erect penis pushing its way between her legs. He began to kiss her back finding one of her erogenous zones on her neck and inner thighs, she too was getting excited. After a little foreplay they made passionate love for quite a while and Samantha felt that they had reached new heights. The relationship appeared to be better and Samantha felt less inhibited as she experimented with new positions becoming more adventurous than on previous occasions. His idea to impersonate Dracula seemed to excite her the most, as fear seemed to excite her and she reached an orgasmic level in no time at all. Her fantasy was not rape related but anything that potentially scared her also turned her on, usually horror movies and being close to death appealed to her sexually, maybe it was related to being comforted after being scared. The sense of security that she needed to feel belonged, and not a sexual vessel that was used and thrown away; or a discarded love doll abandoned by men who merely want sex and not commitment. The rest of that night proved uneventful as they lay naked together sleeping and at peace, neither had spoken but used their bodies to express what they wanted to say.

The next day they spent researching myths and legends in the study, they also contacted Fiona and Harrison giving them an update about the mirrors and their relationship.

Fiona was particularly interested in Samantha and Elliot as it had been a love hate relationship in the past, also like most woman she liked a good romance with a happy ending.

Later that evening Elliot was talking in Samantha's room

"So are you happy about this assignment?" Elliot asked.

"Am I fuck, it stinks but what can we do?" Samantha said.

"I thought we had solved the mirror thing!" Elliot said confused.

"Yes well according to Daniel we still had issues and the Harrington Curse went deeper into the origins of Mexico. We only knew what Annabelle told us and what the Ralph's diary revealed, but there was another story which Daniel will investigate in due course going back to Aztec history."

Samantha and Elliot had discovered another mirror in the study and even traced the history of Captain Alvarado's family to the modern family which had dwindled down to a few. The curse had evidently found them and destroyed most of them, on investigation they discovered that a lot of them had gruesome deaths. Babies drowning, mothers and babies dying during child birth, horrific fires and car crashes. There were reports of choking on blood, deaths at work, amputations and decapitations. It would be enough to put you off eating for life thinking about the gruesome deaths, on each occasion a mirror was in the household of at least one member of the family. Although Elliot was aware of all the details regarding these deaths it still failed to deter him from his incredible appetite.

"Stuart must you eat that baguette like you haven't eaten for ages?"

"But Sammy, I haven't I was whisked off suddenly practically starving!"

"For fuck sake Stuart I'm hungry too but I don't eat like a monster!" Samantha said frowning.

"So why is Ruth the nurse joining us?" Elliot asked.

"This is so that we can distinguish reality from fantasy!" Samantha said sighing at Elliot's lack of understanding.

"You mean fact from fiction, good idea." Elliot agreed.

"Emma will also be there to witness events." Samantha anticipated the same response from Elliot

"Emma Harrington?" Elliot asked "In connection with the mirrors?"

"Yes Emma Harrington she offered to help us." Samantha replied

"And we have read about the Alvarado family so why are you asking about the mirrors when they are the reason behind so much tragedy?" Samantha explained. "God Elliot how do you get by in life, nothing sinks in that tiny mind of yours!"

Samantha was on form as usual with her sarcastic remarks and Elliot just responded with his usual shrugging of the shoulders and continued researching the Alvarado family history. Soon after Samantha went over to him with a coy look and full of apologies as if to say why do you put up with me? But Elliot is a tolerant man who takes most things in his stride and occasionally returns the fire, when he does, he shocks Samantha. His approach is pretty effective demonstrating a controlled use of verbal missiles that each hit the target with amazing accuracy.

"Elliot I am sorry but you really don't understand the whole family curse thing do you?" Samantha sat beside Elliot with her arm around his waist.

"Quite frankly I don't." Elliot admitted.

"Then allow me to explain." Samantha said smiling. "Captain Alvarado couldn't understand the romance between Domingo Fierro, one of his best sailors and Zyanya the Aztec witch. Alvarado had never loved anyone not even his dear mother and so he considered that you only married for reproduction purposes after all they had big families back then. Also why get involved with a witch; was he under her spell, a victim of her evil charms? Remember he was wounded and weak susceptible to her charms, that's not to say that she was evil like the Spanish want us to believe, perhaps she really did love him."

"Sammy I know about the wounds inflicted on him from some sort of creature like a Panther, but wasn't she supposed to be capable of transforming herself into a wild beast?"

"Yes ancient history suggests that Aztec witches could transform themselves into animals such as Panthers." Samantha replied. "But that's fiction or mythology and we are researching facts about the family and the mirrors."

"And one fact is the spontaneous human combustion the Captain was said to have died due to this and so have many other cases since this incident or accident whichever way you view it." Elliot felt proud having produced his own evidence of events as follows.

SPONTANEOUS HUMAN COMBUSTION

Human spontaneous combustion or people setting alight in flames for no apparent reason - it was said that Captain Gonzalo Alvarado died this way in his cabin. The surviving crew members witnessed the event and watched the ship burn later that night it was said to be horrific like someone setting light to him.

Frank Clarke died in this way just set alight for no apparent reason; the last thing he saw was the flaming eyes of Zyanya, demonstrating the power of such a vengeful witch. Yet she was causing harm to innocent people whom she would never have done consciously, but the curse continued to cause problems all over the world. His daughter Pepper Clarke an eighteen year old girl with long blonde hair soft complexion and a slim figure remained in the household with her aunt

Gail and cousin Jasmin hoping to find out the cause of her father's death disbelieving in curses, myths or legends.

Spontaneous human combustion is a widely known phenomenon that cannot be explained but occurs in similar ways in each case. The body sets alight suddenly and with no rational explanation, various theories are brought forward from scientist and other professionals some lead to a dehydrated body with the right combustible chemicals in their body and it takes something to ignite it causing devastating effects.

Elliot had put his case across and completely astounded Samantha who could only reply with, "Okay."

That night things really did happen as Samantha and Elliot lay in bed, they heard a blood curdling scream they both leapt out of bed put on their dressing gowns and ran to the door. They noticed their light flicker and the door was stuck, Elliot began pulling at it and finally they opened it and ran across the corridor and down the stairs. Further noises came from the study, they entered wearily, and Elliot was clutching a torch while Samantha grabbed a candle stick. As they entered they noticed Olivia spinning in mid air as if she was in a whirlwind, sprays of glass surrounded her and Marie was swept up and got pinned to the door by two daggers buried in her shoulders. Elliot looked in the mirror and saw a floating head, he removed his gown and threw it over the mirror and Olivia dropped to the ground. They managed to free Maria from the door and heard shouting from the kitchen as Carlos was trying to get Margo up from the floor; Carlos was in shock he had blood on his hands. Samantha looked down at Margo, she was bleeding.

"I thought I saw a snake on the floor and so I stabbed it with my knife!" He said shaking.

"It was me Carlos I was tossed to the ground by a wild cat, like a black panther, he must have seen that and stabbed me instead of the cat!" Margo said.

Samantha and Elliot managed to keep the mirror covered and did the same to the other mirror which was hanging close by. They told the family to keep it safe until it could be parcelled up for export back to Mexico. Soon after this they left for the airport and made plans to travel home.

FINDING THE MIRRORS

Harrison was in Mexico where he met a tour guide called Catherina as he had already discovered links to the cave and volcano that was Zyanya's dwelling place for many years. He followed an English group of tourists who were being guided by an attractive and confident Spanish woman called Catherina. She spoke perfect English and appeared well dressed and kept her dark hair loose, blowing about in the breeze. She seemed to be attracted to Harrison each time she spoke she glanced at Harrison and smiled, Harrison noticed and felt confident enough to ask her out on a date. Unfortunately Fiona wasn't present to advise him to take care and to look into her background; Fiona was like his older sister seeking to protect him. Harrison felt like a school boy again discovering love for the first time, he had to admit to himself that he was smitten once more, captured by her charms.

Catherina was slim and had dark tanned skin which was as natural as her radiant smile; she had long dark hair that trailed down her slender back. She was smartly dressed in a white blouse and skirt, her skin shone like silk. Harrison was immediately attracted to her and gasped as he tried to speak to her, he had a million questions to ask her but one important one. He wanted to date her and tried to find the courage to ask her, he had lost his confidence since his last girl friend left him.

Eventually he found himself alone in a room with her and began to discuss the history behind the Aztec people.

"I could do with finding out more about Zyanya the witch." Harrison began.

"You know about her?" Catherina said surprised.

"Yes a little from researching the web." Harrison explained.

"Well if you wanted to know more I'm your woman." She said.

"Okay maybe over dinner perhaps?" Harrison continued.

"Yes of course." Catherina replied her hazel eyes sparkled under the lights.

"Can we meet tonight?" Harrison asked eagerly.

"Yes of course that would be lovely." Catherina said smiling.

Harrison felt himself getting hot and sweating under his shirt, he was experiencing blushing for the first time in his life. Little did he know but Catherina was going through a similar experience as she was talking to him, she was actually quaking inside feeling sick and anxious. Harrison had been in action abroad in the Army and never felt as anxious as he did when he was talking to her.

"Until tonight then?" Catherina offered her hand in friendship.

"Yes." Harrison replied shaking her hand gently.

Harrison began to walk towards the exit when he heard her call.

"I don't know your name!" she shouted.

"Daniel Harrison. And you?" He asked.

"Catherina." She replied. "I will pick you from your hotel at seven."

"It's the Tequila." He said stumbling on his words.

"Okay bye." She said waving her hand.

Later that evening Harrison was ready to meet Catherina, he was pacing up and down the lobby of the hotel. He was dressed in a casual suit and was wearing a thick layer of deodorant and after shave. Smelling fresh and clean, feeling confident that he would get on well with her. Meanwhile Catherina was running later preparing herself to meet him, spending time in the shower and putting on her make up. She took a long time deciding what to wear for her date; clothes came out of the wardrobe and returned there until she found the right dress to wear in order to impress him. She then found the most expensive perfume and sprayed it on liberally so she didn't intoxicate him. Harrison was still pacing when her car arrived to pick him up, by this time he was getting anxious thinking that she wouldn't turn up. What he failed to understand was that women take longer than men to get ready, this is a well known fact but not to him. It's all about looking the part and feeling confident that she is presentable and above all in this case desirable.

Catherina stepped out of the car looking radiant as if she had stepped off the front cover of Vogue magazine or a catwalk. She even had the walk of a model.

"Hello Daniel." She said cheerfully. "Sorry I'm late."

"Oh that's okay." Harrison replied gasping. "I must say you're stunning!"

"Why thank you!" She said smiling. "You look very nice too."

"Get in the car and we can find a restaurant." She said opening the passenger door to her red Ferrari.

She drove away and pointed out a few historical places on route, they eventually stopped at an Italian restaurant. Catherina parked the car and they walked towards the restaurant arm in arm as if they had been dating for a while. When they got inside a waiter took them to a suitable table and asked them if they wanted a drink, Daniel chose a bottle of white wine and they settled down for their meal.

"Well this is nice Daniel." Catherina said looking around the room.

"Yes delightful." He replied. "And please call me Danny or Dan."

"Okay Dan, what do you want to know about Zyanya?" she asked.

"Everything you know." he replied.

"That will take all night!" she said.

"I've got all night, have you?" He said confidently.

"That depends on how we get on!" She replied equally as confident.

Their meals arrived before long and they began eating spaghetti and drinking wine, little conversation occurred at this time just the usual getting to know you questions. Where are you from? And what do you do in your spare time but nothing could prepare Harrison for this night. He expected an informative conversation and a goodnight kiss but got much more than he bargained for. Catherina could be regarded as a seducer and a dominant woman who enjoyed the type of masosadist love making, he was only used to the conventional method that was a little safer. In fact when he took out holiday insurance it didn't include painful sex acts that could potentially put you in traction.

Later that evening Catherina took him back to her lavish apartment and asked him to sit on the settee, she went into the bedroom and returned wearing a basque and holding a whip. His face expressed exactly what he felt anxiety and dread but also somewhat bewildered by such a transformation from an innocent looking girl to a cat woman look alike. She even had cat's ears to match her outfit. She led him into the bedroom and told him to remove his clothes; once he was naked she tied him to the bed smiling as she did so.

"Now Danny, I will tell you all about Zyanya after we make love!" she explained.

She proceeded to whip him but not harshly, and then she applied lubricating gel all over his body mainly on his penis. She could see that she was exciting him as his penis was already erect, so she played with it for a while and then tied a piece of cotton to it.

"What's that for?" He asked.

"It's in order to maintain your erection big boy!" She said starting to strip naked.

Her shapely breasts appeared over the top of the Basque and she began to use the gel on them rubbing at her nipples and then forcing one of them into his mouth, then she undid the buttons close to her vagina and lifted it up rubbing herself on his stomach. She began to moan and kissed his lips gently then bit his lips licking away the blood after a while she began to flow like a fountain over his chest. He could only lie down and take the punishment that she offered, which was a lot for the information he required. After the prolonged foreplay she remained on top of him and he penetrated her, she was riding him like a horse bearing down tightening her grip on every movement. The entire experience lasted a few hours then she lay beside him, closing her eyes and wiping herself with a towel.

"Can you untie me now please?" He asked.

"Sorry of course I will!" She replied jumping up and removing the ropes.

"Well that was different!" He remarked.

"Yes I usually do more than that but I didn't want to scare you off!" She replied with a wicked grin on her face. "Next time you choose what you want to do!"

Harrison looked at her bronze body shining in the dim light; she had perfect curves and felt as soft as silk next to him. He didn't want to say anything just remember the experience. But he was still curious about the mirrors and Zyanya.

"You were going to tell me about Zyanya." He said.

"Yes sorry I was. I will tell you a story of her life as the Aztec witch, just listen and ask no questions until I finish." She instructed.

Harrison was true to his word and remained silent as she told her story, after all he didn't want to be whipped or punished in any other way, or did he? Catherina told the full story which did take a long time and she appeared to leave nothing out, she even began to cry as she spoke of Zyanya's death and the massacre of so many people. Harrison comforted her and they both fell asleep, later Catherina awoke and began to fidget she was very restless as if she had experienced a nightmare. Harrison slept soundly and undisturbed by her movements, he remained naked with his chest exposed. Catherina went towards a set of draws and opened it quietly, she then took out a dagger and returned to the bed, she gripped the handle with both hands and held it above Harrison's chest; she brought her arms up above her head and held the dagger firmly. Then she looked at him sleeping and dropped the dagger to the ground, picked it up and replaced it in the drawer. After this she got back into bed and hugged him tightly wrapping her legs around his not wanting to let him go.

In the morning they both awoke and Catherina kissed Harrison on the lips, he returned a kiss and felt confident that he was going to have a good day.

"I need to investigate the origins of the mirrors." He said.

"Well breakfast first Danny." She replied. "And then we will investigate the mirrors."

Most of the mirrors were easily traced but some were undetected it was only when Harrison met Catherina that he was able to find the rest with the help from his friends and colleagues. With one combined effort they managed to find each mirror and arrange for them to be returned to Mexico. But this was not without complications as there were reports of planes crashes and ships sinking in various locations.

CAUSE AND EFFECT

All the reporters arrived back at the London office; Fiona arranged a meeting in order to discuss the so called cursed mirrors and the tragedies that were said to be the cause of the mirrors. Fiona chaired the meeting standing at the head of the table to address her colleagues who were sat around the table each with paper and pens in front of them. Ruth Ashley, Emma Harrington and Pepper Clarke joined them. Catherina decided to wait outside in the park; she was sat at a bench observing passers by. A new reporter joined them called Pavina Patel an English girl from Asian parentage who seemed interested in the cursed mirrors and their history. She was small and slim with long black hair. She was well spoken and very pretty with a soft dark complexion.

Fiona looked at everyone each in turn before speaking; she had a look of concern on her face.

"Well we have come a long way with this subject and discovered so much about the mirrors, but we must now stick to the facts and not conjecture. I know that some of the events, accidents, and incidents have been traumatic and hard to understand fully. That's why we have Ruth here to help us stick to reality and differentiate fact from fiction, delusions from hard based facts."

Fiona paused for a while she produced photographs and paperwork concerning the cursed mirrors. "May I ask what you have come up with Dan, as you have just returned from Mexico?"

Harrison stood up and cleared his throat, he seemed confident as he produced his own paperwork and photographs from his suitcase.

"Ladies and gentlemen may I introduce to you the Aztec witch Zyanya, she is the key to our investigations." He held up a picture for all to see. "I have been trying to find the cave where she once lived and the volcano close by but so far nothing. I have been assisted by a descendant of hers called Catherina; she is a tour guide in Mexico and knows a great deal about Zyanya. We worked closely on the background story of Zyanya and the love story surrounding a Sailor called Domingo Fierro. He was apparently wounded by a Panther and was discovered by Zyanya who escorted him into a cave. She nursed him back to health which took a while as he had developed a fever, she used potions and herbs for medicine and eventually he became well again. As he gathered his strength back he got to know Zyanya as an attractive, kind and considerate person, who he soon fell in love with. She was equally in love with him and wanted him to stay with her, but he was worried that his fellow sailors might search for him and discover her cave. Zyanya had riches there that they would no doubt take and so he decided to leave and return to the ship, reporting to Captain Alvarado. On his return he was questioned about his wounds and who had cared for him, but Fierro only told him about being helped by the Aztec people. After this he was being watched by another admirer, a Spanish girl called Andora Martinez who wanted to marry him and often flirted with him in front of the ships crew. He had made a few trips to the cave to see Zyanya and they made love there, unaware that Andora was close by and she reported back to Captain Alvarado, She did it out of jealousy not wanting to get Fierro into trouble but to have Zyanya captured and killed. She had hoped that after her death that he may fall in love with her and forget the one she termed as an evil witch. She also believed that he was under her spell and her evil charms caused him to love her. At least that's what she told Alvarado who would believe her as he hated the Aztec people and wanted to be honoured by his people back in Spain for destroying the Aztec culture and faith. It so happened that the captain, killed thousands of Aztecs and stole their treasure and land. He then flogged and executed Zyanya and put Fierro in chains. After this it would seem that the captain returned to his ship went into his cabin and was witnessed to burst into flames like spontaneous human combustion. It was witnessed by Estaban Gallego the cabin boy who survived the following tragedy, which was described as some kind of whirlwind on the ship. This strange phenomenon caused chaos for the crew and led to their deaths, even Andora was found hanging from one of the masts having been launched into the air by a rope that was stuck around her neck she died of asphyxiation or a lack of oxygen to the body by choking. Fierro survived along with the cabin boy, they swam to shore as the ship caught fire, no one can explain how he broke free from the chains. So many things happened at once and some of the crew experienced horrendous deaths, being cut down by swords and spikes embedded in their heads". Harrison paused "And that brings us to the present, as I explained I have tried to find the cave and I will be returning to Mexico with Catherina to continue searching."

"Thank you for enlightening us Dan at least we know the full story. Now Samantha would you like to add anything?"

"Yes both Stuart and I went to Spain and found the descendants of Captain Alvarado; the family had met many fates including amazingly enough spontaneous human combustion. Adults and children had met their fate in many ways from drowning, road traffic accidents and falling from buildings. While, I might add these deaths were not said to have been through suicide, or suspicious circumstances or even foúl play. It is strange that so many tragedies should occur in one family in such a short space of time, I can only concur that some kind of evil was around like the Harrington family had experienced."

"This sounds amazing I would love to see something like that, it is legendary?" Pavina said looking at Fiona.

"Let's not get carried away here Sammy, remember we deal in facts." Fiona reminded Samantha and all the others attending the meeting.

"May I say that we have experienced many things some which could be explained away, but you can't rule out the possibility of evil and the paranormal?" Elliot said supporting Samantha.

"Stuart really we can't publish a series of paranormal events that we have witnessed but can't prove, we would be laughed at by the public and our credibility would be in tatters." Fiona insisted.

"It's all about cause and effect, we witnessed one thing call it a mass hallucination if you like. The cause could have been some kind of chemical imbalance like the mirrors in the Harrington household that contained a drug powerful enough to cause hallucinations or something in the food or drink who knows." Ruth said pausing for a reaction "The cause was the drug and the reaction or effect was hallucinations, delusions and illusions, and mirrors playing mind games. The way I see it is we all need closure with this and the only way is to go to Mexico and destroy the mirrors, only then can we put an end to this business. As for the article we can offer various explanations and leave the reader to decide what caused all the misery, just a thought Fi." Ruth said looking around the room as everyone applauded.

"Nice one Ruth." Samantha said smiling.

Elliot nodded and Pepper stood to her feet still clapping, then she looked at Fiona. "So are we all going to Mexico?" She asked in a soft voice.

"Yes I suppose so, Samantha and Stuart with Emma, followed by Ruth, Pepper and myself." Fiona turned to Harrison. "You will no doubt be going back tomorrow with Catherina?"

"Yes I thought I would see if I could find the cave." Harrison said smiling.

"Good idea then we can dispose of the mirrors in the volcano and hopefully lift the curse."

Harrison called Elliot to one side. "Could I have a private word?"

Samantha noticed them disappear out of the room and was curious what Harrison had to say. So she followed them out of the room and noticed them heading to the toilet. She lingered outside hoping to hear them from outside, but all she could here was mumbling.

"Stuart listen I need to tell you something." Harrison began.

"Okay you have my attention." Elliot said concerned.

Harrison removed his shirt and revealed scratch marks on his front and back, he also had nasty bites on his body.

"What the hell is that?" Elliot shouted. "My god have you been attacked?"

"Yes by Christina." Harrison replied.

"Oh you mean like sexually?" Elliot was baffled.

"Yes she's a sadomasochist and I found out the hard way!" Harrison admitted.

"Do you like that sort of thing?" Elliot asked curiously.

"No of course not but what can I do?" Harrison said asking for his advice.

"I really don't know, but you need to do something it's dangerous." Elliot replied trying to find an answer to Harrison's dilemma.

"Don't tell anyone. I need to sort this out." Harrison said putting his shirt back on.

Harrison told Elliot everything about the claws and hoods, bondage and all he was able to remember about the traumatic events.

Later that night Samantha and Elliot were lying in bed, having just made love, Elliot had trouble performing because of what Harrison had showed him and discussed about his sex life.

"Okay Stuart, tell me about Danny." she insisted.

"Danny?" Elliot said puzzled.

"Oh, so he pulled you to one side for nothing and he took you into the toilet for a chat. Then he came out doing his shirt buttons up like he had been showing you something, come on Stuart I'm not fucking stupid!" Samantha said annoyed.

"Oh that!" Elliot said.

"Yes that, now tell me about it." Samantha said looking into his eyes. "And remember I know when you're fucking lying."

"His girlfriend is into sadomasochism and she has caused him many injuries in the process of love making, it's like a ritual of some kind." Elliot explained.

"Sadomasochism!"

"Oh, you mean you have done it or……" Elliot was interrupted.

"Fuck off Stuart, I mean I know about it through books and the internet." Samantha seemed angry at his remark.

"I just thought." Elliot tried to reason with her.

"No Stuart I am not dressing up in costumes and performing with whips and that sort of thing so you can forget that!" Samantha made it obvious that she did hear a few things. "Wearing hoods and using claws!"

"Wait I never told you that, were you listening in?" Elliot asked.

"I may have listened in at some point!" Samantha replied.

"You mean outside the toilet?" Elliot asked.

"Well maybe I entered the door!" Samantha paused. "Well I was curious!"

"So don't tell anyone, okay?" Elliot insisted.

"Not me." Samantha simulated pulling a zip across her mouth. "Zip my lips are sealed."

Later that day Samantha and Fiona were sat in the office, Samantha did her usual tidy up regime, everything in its place and double checking it was tidy and all her items matched in colour. This was to the annoyance of Fiona who had piles of papers on her desk and none of her office equipment matched in colour.

"You clearly have an OCD problem." Fiona said looking through her papers.

"I do?" Samantha replied.

"Yes, obsessive compulsive disorder." Fiona said. "Where is that last report on Zyanya?"

"I know what it means and I can't fucking help it." Samantha replied.

"You mean like your swearing?" Fiona said smiling.

"Sorry, I really don't know when I am doing it, bloody annoying." Samantha smiled back.

"Sammy you're one of a kind." Fiona suddenly jumped up. "Found it!"

"Jesus, Fi you frightened me, what the fucks wrong?" Samantha asked.

"I was looking for this report on the history of Zyanya for my story." Fiona explained. "I'm piecing the facts together based on all your reports so far."

"Fi?" Samantha said hesitating.

Fiona looked at her puzzled sitting back down at her desk. "Yes Sammy what is it?"

"I need to tell you something about Danny." Samantha said glancing at the door.

"Well, tell me!" Fiona said eagerly.

"He has a problem." Samantha hesitated again feeling awkward.

"Is it a drink problem or what?" Fiona asked. "Look Danny and I go back a long way I would know if he had a problem."

"Believe me, this is a problem!" Samantha continued. "It's to do with that tour guide he's seeing."

"Really?" Fiona seemed abrupt.

"Yes she is into sadomasochism and he is cut, scratched and bitten, she has bound him and put a hood over his head too!" Samantha was so relieved that she had told her.

"No, it can't be true!" Fiona said shocked. "Who told you Danny?"

"No, it was Stuart, Danny told him in confidence." Samantha said.

"My god, I can hardly believe this!" Fiona said looking down at her papers.

"I know it's bad." Samantha agreed.

"No this report about Zyanya from your trip to Spain." Fiona paused to think. "Is he sure about the facts from Danny about Christina?"

At that moment Elliot entered the room and looked at the expression on Fiona's face, Fiona had a very expressive face that anyone could read easily, they could tell what mood she was in by the look she gave them.

"Fi?" Elliot said reluctantly expecting a bad response.

"You had better have the facts right on Danny." Fiona said angrily.

"Sammy you told Fi what I said?" Elliot said shocked.

“Sorry Stuart but Fi needed to know.” Samantha said in her own defence “We care you know and stick together as a team.”

“Yes I did Stuart and you should have told me.” Fiona said.

At that point Harrison entered the room; he felt the hostility in the air and looked at each one of them.

“It’s about me isn’t it?” He said looking at Elliot.

“I had to tell them Danny it’s serious.” Elliot admitted.

“It’s okay Stuart I would have told Fi anyway.” Harrison admitted.

“Can we have a moment alone?” Fiona asked.

Samantha and Elliot left the room swiftly and closed the door behind them.

“Danny we have known each other for many years and I know you’re in danger with this woman, please listen before it’s too late.” Fiona warned him.

“I know Fi but I am okay.” Harrison reassured her.

“You don’t enjoy that do you?” Fiona asked concerned.

“No! Of course not!” Harrison said surprised at her question. “I like safe sex and that’s not safe, being ravaged by a cat or bitten by a wild cat.”

“I will speak to her about it.” Harrison said confidently.

Samantha reflected back on her years with Criminal world, she began to wonder whether or not she had been selfish, unfeeling or unhelpful. No one suggested that she never cared and as far as she was concerned she protected others like Ruth Ashley the nurse who she hated at first. The reason that she thought of this was because Fiona had made a remark about Elliot protecting Harrison. It was on her mind and she constantly thought about it ever since, she had also considered how badly she treated Elliot and wanted to make up for her behaviour in some way, but she still wouldn't dress up to do this, kinky sex wasn't her style. She was concerned that Harrison could be harmed by the sadomasochistic lover and wanted to help him, but her hand were tied and not in a literal sense! What no one was aware of was that Catherina had attempted to stab him in the chest with a dagger on a few occasions mostly when he was wearing a hood. These incidents were without provocation and the exact reason wasn't known at this point, but it was clear that he was in danger and that she really did have mental health issues. To launch at someone with a claw, making wild cat sounds and biting him has to be bizarre, but to try to stab him to death shows her unstable state of mind.

Catherina and Harrison travelled around the England collecting mirrors and sending them back to Mexico, they did the same in the United States of America while the others travelled to the other countries finding more mirrors and returning them to an address that Harrison gave them in Mexico. Some mirrors were hard to track down but with the help from the media, radio and television announcements they were found. Once Harrison had completed his task he was to return to Mexico.

Samantha and Elliot had lunch with Ruth and a very bewildered Pepper, the innocent blonde girl who had recently lost her father through the cursed mirrors at her home. She was fascinated by the investigation into the curse of Zyanya, so much so that she insisted on being involved in the investigations. She became very close to Fiona who kept her well informed, everyone was so kind to her and helped her in any way they could. Pavina was also present in order to learn more about their journey.

While they were planning their journey back to Mexico sitting round a large table the conversation was about Ruth as Pepper wanted to know about Ruth's girl friend Pamela who died so tragically.

"So have you always been gay?" Pepper asked.

"I once had boyfriends but it never worked out, I suppose I always knew that I was gay." Ruth said.

"So what is lesbian sex like?" Elliot asked. "I mean I know about heterosexual sex between a man and a woman, but I don't get lesbian sex?"

"Stuart really that's personal!" Samantha said disgusted with him.

"Yes Stuart don't be so insensitive." Fiona remarked.

"It's okay I really don't mind educating Stuart. It's all about the emotions, hormones raging and sensual sex that is only experienced by two women. The love is tender and sweet based on deep feelings and not wham bam thank you mam as men are accustomed to. Foreplay is the main part and the kissing is longer and tender using tongues and sometimes equipment or sex toys."

"Wow that's amazing!" Stuart remarked.

"Thank you for understanding Stuart." Ruth replied.

"So did you find it hard being accepted in society?" Pavina asked.

"Yes by some people usually religious leaders or fanatics, Catholics and Muslims mainly they believe that we are evil. Although Priests are some of the worst child abusers they use religion to lure children into a false sense of security and abuse them.

"I read the article 'Cracked Porcelain' and noticed that that was about abuse." Pepper said concerned.

"Yes it was about Pamela mainly as she was cracked porcelain; she was a beautiful child who was abused by her uncle. She was as beautiful as a porcelain mask or vase and became cracked porcelain when she was sexually abused and later in life raped. I am like cracked porcelain because I was abused as a child, its something you never forget. At first I felt dirty and worthless, and then I felt it was my fault for allowing it to happen. You go through a lot of emotions much like mourning and then you get nightmares and a sickness in your stomach that cannot be described, I suppose its like knots in your abdomen and you physically vomit. I don't like crowds because I hate people invading my personal space; I am not tactile and react to the smell of some after shaves. I hate fat chubby men who wear glasses and have bald heads as I remember my abuser looked like that." Ruth began to have tears in her eyes.

"Sorry Ruth, have I upset you?" Pepper asked.

"No you haven't sweet child, but what does upset me is when the bastards who abuse others or the predators get away with it." Ruth said angrily.

"The fuckers ought to be castrated with a rusty knife!" Samantha shouted making Stuart jump.

"Well when you suffer for the rest of your life its true there is no justice, it makes you wonder who is being punished!" Pepper said watching Ruth rushing out of the room to the toilet.

"Thank you Stuart so fucking diplomatic." Samantha said going after Ruth.

When Samantha entered the toilet Ruth was being sick, Samantha stood outside the cubical.

"Sorry about Stuart, he never thinks before he speaks." Samantha said.

"It doesn't matter Sammy its something I have to deal with." Ruth replied wiping her mouth with a tissue.

The next day they all went to the airport and awaited their flight to Mexico, Pavina was invited to join them so that she could learn more about Criminal World and their investigations. Ruth had a panic attack after a man swept past her looking like her abuser. Pepper comforted her along with Samantha who hurled abuse at him for upsetting Ruth.

"You daft bastard who do you think you are?" Samantha shouted.

"Are you sure Ruth is well enough for this journey?" Pavina asked.

"Yes, she is stronger than you think." Samantha said. "She has been through a lot in thirty years, she can cope."

"I have and I can also fight my own battles I am no fucking wimp!" Ruth said.

"Sorry Ruth I just wanted to help." Samantha said.

"Chilax Sammy I was joking!" Ruth said smiling.

"I like that word Ruth, chillax it sounds awesome!" Pepper said chuckling.

"Chilax is that even a word?" Pavina said puzzled.

"Is it fuck? I combined chill and relax to form chillax!" Ruth said. "I use it on the psyche ward along with climaxical and smilaff!" Ruth explained.

"Fucking works for me!" Samantha said.

"What on earth is climaxical?" Pepper asked.

"Controlling your emotions and modifying reactions." Ruth explained.

"Is that like faking an orgasm?" Samantha said jokingly.

"Yes sort of." Ruth replied. "It's known as having a climaxical moment!"

"What about smilaff, what the fucks that about?" Pepper asked.

"Now that's when you try not to laugh and smile tongue in cheek." Ruth said demonstrating the sound and actions. "Not easy to do."

Everyone laughed and failed to notice Fiona coming back from the information desk.

"Right ladies I have the flight details here and our destination." Fiona said holding up some relevant papers.

Pavina seemed to work out the details very fast and planned the route without any problem; she seemed to know the airport well and escorted them all to the right departure lounge.

"How did you know the way?" Fiona asked.

"My sister Pretty is a stewardess on one of the airlines and I spent time travelling to various destinations in my work as a journalist."

BACK IN MEXICO

Harrison flew back to Mexico with Catherina on the way over he discussed his plan with her; he wanted to destroy the mirrors in the volcano. Catherina seemed reluctant to assist him to find the cave as if it still obtained treasure and secrets never to be revealed. Yet Ralph the artist had been there as he discussed with her and he brought back knowledge of the Aztec race, including drawings and small objects.

Harrison had made a discovery of his own which led him to be concerned when he first went to Mexico, when he first met Catherina. He found the cave of Zyanya and found paintings of soldiers and other artefacts he noticed a resemblance between him and Domingo Fierro and realised that the legend of Fierro was true Zyanya did love the soldier. This also meant that this was the volcano that the mirrors had come from, made from volcanic lava. Harrison was excited about his discovery; he wanted to tell Catherina, he knew that she would be equally excited to find her family home, or at least the ancestor that she admired so much.

Before the others arrived from England, Harrison put together a map of the area, this included volcano's and known caves within the area. Catherina was again reluctant to help as if she wanted to avoid the cave; maybe she was frightened of the unknown and just wanted to get on with her life.

Harrison had further sexual experiences following the similar rituals with claws, costumes and finally the hood where she took out the dagger from a draw and tried to stab him. Something always stopped her as if she wasn't meant to kill him, but why did she try if this was the case. The only thing he needed to know now was where the location of the cave and volcano where Zyanya lived. It was a calm evening that followed a hectic day, as Harrison had been racing around everywhere searching for the cave where Zyanya the witch once lived. He knew he was close when he saw a volcano that had produced the mirrors that had caused so many problems for so many people. Maybe if these mirrors were returned it would put an end to the terrible curse that was attached to these mirrors. Harrison and his friends had witnessed too much suffering and just wanted to see an end to it all, they had witnessed the loss of some of the Harrington family and now all they wanted was closure. Harrison appeared exhausted and a little bewildered by Catherina's actions as she seemed to sanction Zyanya's action, knowing the moral and ethical implications behind what she did. Catherina seemed confused by her ancestors lifestyle and argued that she acted in the best interest of her people, her death by execution and its implications on her race helped to support her argument, but the curse could not be justified as a vengeful act as innocent people were harmed and killed.

Harrison used his torch to search for the entrance to the cave, he was convinced that he would come to no harm as the mirrors didn't appear to see him as a threat and he was only thrown across the room because he got in the way of others. That was at least his own rational for his survival and he could have been killed several times in the past when he was trying to retrieve the mirrors. For someone who kept an open mind Harrison was certainly convinced that the mirrors were cursed and needed to be destroyed. But had he been led into a false sense of security? He loved Catherina and like Fierro could have been charmed into submission, falling in love with a woman that had the power to control him with her affections and seduce his mind into submission.

Harrison set out to find the cave where Zyanya once lived; he didn't inform his friend because he considered that he would not come to any harm as the mirrors didn't consciously attack him and he may be able to return the mirrors without any problem. That at least was his theory and one that made sense at the time, in his eyes he was protecting his friends from danger and trying to end the curse.

Harrison found a series of branches covering what seemed to be an entrance to a cave, as he pulled the branches away he revealed a small entrance. He entered cautiously watching the inner part widening until he noticed a tunnel. On the walls he noticed paintings each one told its own story about the Spanish arriving in Mexico on ships and of the terrible massacre of the Aztec people. Everything fell into place and Harrison began to understand, he took pictures with his phone and then with his camera. Then he noticed more recent pictures that indicated that someone was still living in the cave. He saw a man being sacrificed to the Aztec gods and a lot of blood spilt, he then noticed the picture of a mirror being carried to a lake inside a cave like dwelling. Volcanic lava no doubt Harrison thought to himself, maybe this is here to indicate the destruction of mirrors, but who painted the pictures?

Harrison's thoughts were disturbed by a noise which echoed down the tunnel, it was the sound of foot steps. He found a place to hide behind a rock, he listened again, but all was silent then he smelt a strange substance and before long he felt himself go dizzy and faint eventually he passed out.

Harrison's friends and colleagues were in a hotel room working out the local area using maps and information gathered by local people. It was Pavina that worked out the route to each cave and discovered volcanoes in the area, she was clever as well as pretty, her mind was sharp and she could work things out logically. But she was also modest and tried not to take all the credit for finding the caves, she just wanted to help and be part of the team as the newest member of Criminal World magazine. The one problem Pavina had was fitting into her new surroundings, although she appeared confident she was a little nervous and shy. She had faced racial abuse at school and in her working environment and had hoped for a new start as a reporter in Criminal World. Samantha was over confident and never had a problem mixing apart from her abrupt manner and vulgar tongue. The differences were astounding but they seemed to get on well, Pavina admired Samantha's boldness.

SACRIFICE

When Harrison awoke he found himself tied up and lying across a large flat rock which was flat like a concrete slab. He recognised the place from one of the paintings; it was a large opening with a lake in the centre. A pool of lava and the area was lit by many lanterns; it was a wonder to behold as were the painting in the cave. But why was he here in this place and who had brought him to this spot and bound him with ropes? He couldn't see anyone close by and he began to shout out.

"Hello, is anyone there?" Harrison shouted loudly.

Suddenly he saw the figure of a woman faintly in the distance he recognised her shapely figure, it was Catherina. He then focused on her face, and he again looked back at the strange clothes that she was wearing. She was dressed in a period costume like the Aztec witch Zyanya.

"Thank god, it's you, now you can untie me." Harrison said in relief.

"No. I can't do that." Catherina replied.

She was holding a long pointed dagger in her hand and approached him walking very slowly, it was the dagger that she had at her apartment in her drawer.

"What do you mean no? You have a knife, cut the ropes!" Harrison instructed.

"You are to be sacrificed and this is my dagger." Catherina said staring like someone in a trance.

"Okay what's wrong, is this some kind of joke? Harrison said looking around for a camera or a crowd of friends having a prank.

"Catherina let me go!" Harrison insisted.

"Don't call me Catherina!" She shouted angrily holding the dagger to his throat. "I am Zyanya the powerful witch leader of the Aztec nation, reaping revenge on those who tried to destroy me."

"Now I know you're mad!" Harrison said feeling the cold steel blade of the dagger against his flesh. "Careful that looks sharp."

"It is sharp, believe me." Catherina said cutting a piece of rope without any effort.

"Did you say I was to be sacrificed?" Harrison said nervously.

"Yes my love, it's necessary so that we might be together forever." She explained. "I am Zyanya and I am immortal, you are my lover and I want you to be with me forever in my world."

"Look I think you have been slightly misinformed, you are not Zyanya and you're certainly not immortal!" Harrison was trying to reason with her attempting to reach her mind and jolt what was left of her sanity.

"Trust me I am immortal but you will only believe me when you die and you are resurrected into the next life." She said stroking his face with the back of her hand.

"What if I don't want to die or be with you forever?" Harrison said.

"Oh but my darling you do." She said kissing his cheek and then his lips.

She stood up and turned towards the lake signalling people who were dressed similar to her.

"Come forth and let us begin the ceremony!" She beckoned with her right hand raised holding the knife.

Suddenly the area was filled with people and they all began to chant, each one wearing feathers in their head dress and a multitude of colours on their costumes, and the faces of animals on medallions. All of them seemed as if they were on some kind of drug that helped them to act out this strange ritual. Nothing seemed real not even to Harrison who lay with his bare chest exposed to the elements awaiting his death. All he could do was lie there wishing his friends would come and rescue him, but he never told them where he was going; foolishly he had kept it a secret. He wanted to surprise his friends and destroy the mirrors without putting them in danger. Now he was regretting ever thinking of leaving them out and he was paying the price with his life.

The chanting continued as Catherina stood in front of Harrison watching his chest rise and fall, she began to count his respirations; at twenty respirations a minute she seemed happy that he was ready to be sacrificed. So she lifted the dagger like she had done so many times before but this time it was the real thing, the right time to do it and kill Harrison!

“I tried to kill you a few times Danny, when we made love, the first time you were asleep, but I couldn’t do it then. So the second time I got you to wear a hood and then tried again and again but the time wasn’t right either. But now is the time!” She said raising the dagger above her head.

“So all that love making, the sadomasochism was a ritual?” Harrison said.

“Of course it was, it was all in preparation for your death and resurrection.” Catherina explained. “Now get ready to die.”

“No, stop please!” Harrison pleaded.

"I will see you in eternity Danny." Catherina said thrusting the dagger down.

At that moment Catherina was struck on the head by a rock, she appeared dazed at first and dropped the dagger to the floor. There was a lot of confusion as the police had entered the area and were chasing the fleeing people who were dressed as Aztecs. Their ritual was over no one was to be sacrificed. Harrison was being set free by Elliot who had brought Harrison's other friends just in time. Suddenly Catherina got to her feet and picked up the dagger, she made one more attempt to stab Harrison. Samantha noticed her heading towards him and rushed forward to save him.

"No Sammy!" Fiona shouted too far away to stop her.

Samantha was stabbed in the stomach and fell helplessly to the ground, Elliot hit Catherina with his fist and she fell down. She had blood on her temple from the rock that was launched at her and the blood was now trickling down the side of her face.

"Where is your immortality now?" Harrison said getting himself up.

Fiona and Ruth joined them watching helplessly as Elliot knelt beside Samantha. She was clutching her stomach in pain and the blood was oozing through her fingers.

"I feel so cold Stuart." Samantha said.

Everyone was crying watching Samantha as she began to fade away

"Kiss me one last time Stuart." She said as her breathing became shallow.

"Stay with me!" Stuart said feeling Fiona's hand on his shoulder

"I helped someone, I saved Danny." Samantha said in a weak voice. "Now I can see the light, my family are there waiting for me."

"They have come for you Sammy." Ruth said.

"But I am not ready to die!" Samantha said with tears tricking from her eyes.

Pepper and Emma looked around the cave as the lava began to glow lighting up the cave, it was so bright and colourful like something from a fairytale.

"I don't understand, we are not supposed to see the light!" Ruth said.

"What's happening are we all going to die?" Pepper asked.

At that moment a cloud of dust appeared floating over the lava lake, when the dust finally disbursed a head appeared in mid air. It was Zyanya her eyes were glowing and her mouth on fire, she was attractive despite her eyes and flaming tongue.

"Who comes to my home?" She spoke in a powerful voice.

Catherina rose to her feet and walked closer to the lake, she seemed angry and began waving her hands about.

"I am Zyanya not you and I am immortal, I have brought someone to sacrifice to the gods." Catherina said.

"If you claim to be me and are immortal why do you bleed and why do you shame my very name with your actions?" Zyanya said.

"I do not answer to you." Catherina said.

"Then you deserve the punishment that I give to you now." Zyanya said causing a whirlwind to surround Catherina and sweep her into the air; she was then cast into the hot lake to perish. "Now, one of you is hurt."

"She is dead." Ruth said walking forward to the edge of the lake. "She was killed by your descendant Catherina."

"Ruth, come back!" Fiona said concerned.

"She sleeps and I will awaken her." Zyanya said.

"Bring her to the stone bridge, lay her down and leave her." Zyanya commanded.

"Do as she says, I trust her." Ruth instructed.

Harrison and Elliot carried her to the bridge as instructed and lay her on the stone.

"Now go back to the others." Zyanya ordered.

"Do as she says, now!" Ruth shouted.

When they returned a cloud of dust travelled from the lake to the bridge and settled on Samantha, a glow appeared beneath the dust and then disappeared.

"Come and collect her." Zyanya said.

They all rushed to the bridge, Fiona wiped the dust from Samantha's face and her eyes opened. The wound had gone and she smiled at Elliot, he helped her up and they walked away from the bridge.

"Are you alright?" Elliot asked Samantha.

"I feel great, no wound and my skin feels fresh and new!" Samantha said.

"Now get the mirrors and throw them in the lake and then I want you to go and leave me in peace." Zyanya said.

Harrison looked bewildered as they left the cave; all the mirrors were dropped into the lake and were destroyed.

"Danny are you alright?" Fiona asked.

"Yes I am fine, but I feel somehow empty and alone." Harrison said looking at the others. "I let you all down didn't I?"

"No you were very brave." Fiona said.

“But foolish for not telling us where you were going, luckily enough you left us a trail.” Elliot said.

The next day they all went to the airport, when they arrived in England Samantha and Elliot departed first taking Emma home. Fiona and Ruth took Pepper home, returning her to her family. They stayed overnight and then headed south in order to drop Ruth off in her apartment, but as they journeyed home they came across rough weather and Fiona was experiencing problems with her brakes.

“Ruth I am so glad you helped to lift the curse.” Fiona said.

“We all played our part Fi.” Ruth replied modestly.

“I suppose we did, but what team work!” Fiona said smiling.

“Well if ever you need me again let me know.” Ruth offered.

“I will hold you to that Ruth.” Fiona promised.

“I have to say we were lucky to escape alive from that situation.” Ruth said with relief.

“I can’t believe you walked forward and told that witch Zyanya to help us!” Fiona said in amazement.

“I know I amazed myself with that one!” Ruth said smiling.

“The brakes have failed I can’t slow down!” Fiona said panicking.

Fiona pressed again at the foot brake and nothing happened, she was unable to slow down and lost control of the car, she veered off the road and went rolling down a bank and crashing into a ditch. Both Fiona and Ruth appeared pale and lifeless, they sat with their heads to one side, their heads were bleeding. No one was in the area and the car engine was still running with smoke travelling through the air drifting across an open field with no sign of life, not even wild life. Everything remained still, the skies were empty and everything appeared dull as if the life had been taken from the earth leaving nothing but death as a legacy to the world.

CURSED

MASSACRE 27TH JULY 2016

It was one dark rainy evening when a train entered a station few passengers left the train but judging by the horror on the faces of those about to board one of the carriages all was not good. The sounds of screams and people turning away emphasised the degree of horror that they had seen. One of the guard were alerted and he boarded the train firstly he was overcome by a horrible smell and then he saw bodies everywhere with horrific wounds and severed limbs. He was physically sick at the sight of such a massacre; he was soon joined by other guards who alerted the police. Soon after the police arrived with ambulance crew and forensics, people were baffled as rumours of a wild cat or other creature had been on board and killed everybody in the third carriage prior to entering the station. But there was no wild animal present and where could this creature go, they were just left with the carnage it had left behind. Blood stained windows from hands desperately trying to get away, severed limbs on seats and under tables. Battered and bruised torsos with the look of shear horror on their faces, with no one to tell the tale and written on one of the windows of the carriage was the word cursed written in blood.

CURSED INSIDE

It was the middle of summer 2016, the early morning sun was shining brightly, as the sky was clear and blue and it looked like being a wonderful day. Samantha was travelling in her car, heading towards the hospital to visit her colleague and friend Fiona after hearing that she was making a recovery from the car crash. But something didn't seem quite right that morning, Samantha felt odd and acted very strange nothing seemed right since the incident of the cursed mirrors and witnessing Zyanya's remarkable presence. Samantha had supposedly died and been resurrected by Zyanya according to eye witnesses, but Samantha was unsure about their story and questioned the accuracy of each account, She had seen many things since being with criminal world magazine but to believe in such sorcery was beyond what she had considered to be normal or possible.

She had been in a castle owned by Gordon McGregor with equipment that could provide an illusion of ghosts, with visual displays and audible sounds. With trap doors and spooky corridors which enhanced the delusions that she had conjured up in her mind. Yet she survived this and lived to tell the story and since this time experienced many strange things, were they considered hallucinations or delusions brought on by traumatic events? Who can ever say in a world of scientific facts and a history of myths all mixed together to confuse the cleverest of fellows. One thing is for sure they all witnessed Zyanya's appearance and each related the same story word for word, would you call that a mass hallucination?

Both Fiona and Ruth were recovering in hospital; Fiona was kept in for further tests and required a chest x-ray after hitting her chest on the steering wheel. She had been acting strange during her stay in hospital, behaving completely out of character. She was experiencing mood swings and even self harmed in her sleep growling like a lion and scratching her own body. It was reported that Samantha did the same thing a few days before visiting Fiona; she was behaving like Catherina even to the degree of performing pseudo masochistic sexual acts with Elliot. Elliot was shocked and consorted Harrison for advice, he remembered that Harrison had experienced this with Catherina. The use of fancy handcuffs, a whip and a clawed hand during love making hoping to beat Elliot into submission prior to actual penetration. The dominant woman dressed in leather attire and long high healed boots controls her man throughout the performance, but ensure that she leaves the marks on her prey. This is definitely derived from Catherina as part of her desire to become Zyanya and take control as she did over the Aztec race. The power of the spirits or gods who bring light to the earth and bless it with food and sustenance, give life to thousands of people, so they sacrifice life to the gods in return.

Fiona relived the accident in her mind over and over again, Ruth Ashley the psychiatric nurse and herself travelling along when the breaks failed and they went careering out of control down a bank causing chest injuries to Fiona and head injuries to Ruth. Who would have expected such an accident to occur, could this be connected to recent events in Mexico. But surely the curse had been lifted by Zyanya and this was now in the past, Ruth was the main person responsible for the bringing about the end of the curse and the destruction of Catherina the evil descendant of Zyanya, so why did Fiona and Ruth come to harm?

Ruth had been in a coma for days while Fiona was recovering, the porters came to take Fiona for a chest x-ray. They attempted to help her onto a wheelchair but she pushed them away, acting aggressively towards them which seemed out of character for Fiona.

"Get your stinking hands off me you perverts" Fiona said wildly

"Sorry love" Said the one porter

The other porter just stood and stared in disbelief, with his mouth open like a goldfish

"And stop staring at me like I have two heads tosser" Fiona continued

She struggled into the wheelchair showing visual signs of pain on her face and yelling out, but at the same time looking at the porters giving them death stares. Nurse Alesha looked on surprised at Fiona's behaviour she shook her head in disgust and continued with her duties. Fiona was taken down a series of long corridors and in a lift, she arrived at the basement and taken down another corridor and into a room full of machinery. They were greeted by a woman in a white coat who was a little over weight and had her hair tied up neatly in a bun on the top of her head.

"Come over to this machine please" she said politely

"What are you going to do to me?" Fiona asked

"Just take a few x rays that's all" the woman replied

"Watch her Alison she is a bit sharp" One of the porters said

"Take no notice of this pervert, the sick bastard" Fiona said struggling to get in position for her x ray.

"Okay Brian, you can leave us now" Alison said dismissing the porters

Alison began preparing Fiona for her x ray and then disappeared behind the protective screen, she operated the switches.

"Okay hold it" Alison shouted

Fiona took a breath in and held it, but suddenly a flash occurred followed by a bang as the x ray machine exploded and began to smoke, people ran in to find out what was happening. Fiona was found lying on the floor shaking and screaming, Alison was still behind the screen looking shocked by what had occurred. A lot of people in white coats were all centred on Fiona including the porters, who were looking at each other in confusion. Finally nurse Alesha appeared at brushed passed the people and attended to Fiona, she was hesitant at first knowing how she had been towards the porters, but she knew she needed help and obliged her.

"Fiona can you hear me?" she asked concerned

"What is happening to me?" She asked confused.

Alesha leaned over her and smiled "I will help you don't worry"

As Alesha got close to her an item of machinery fell and caused everybody to turn looking across in surprise, meanwhile a spray of dust left Fiona's mouth and entered Alesha causing her to take a deep breath and her eyes to widen and glow. She got up and asked the porters to put her in the wheelchair, they did as they were instructed and wheeled her back to the ward. Alesha then went to help Alison by this time a doctor appeared and also helped her with her recovery.

"Are you alright?" The doctor asked

"Yes of course, but what has happened Dr Phillips?" Alison asked

"Probably some kind of electrical fault Alison, don't worry" Dr Phillips said reassuringly.

Alesha looked at them with strange eyes and then gazed around the room

"If everything is alright I will return to the ward" She said walking towards the door

"I think the X ray may be okay Doctor" one technician announced producing a metal container.

Alesha stopped in her tracks and turned swiftly towards them

"You mean it worked?" Alesha said with a concerned tone in her voice.

"You sound disappointed Alesha?" Dr Phillips said a little bewildered by her reaction.

"No not at all Doctor I was just surprised as the explosion seemed to be so damaging" Alesha said frowning.

Alesha continued to walk away, but still appeared troubled by what had occurred mainly concerning the undamaged X ray film. Fiona returned to her hospital bed she appeared dazed but conscious and allowed the porters to assist her onto the bed.

"Thank you both, its nice to be assisted by two handsome porters" She said smiling.

The men were baffled at such a change in behaviour, it was as if she had a change in personality both of the men shook their heads and smiled.

"Would you credit that John?" Brian said looking at his colleague

"What's up Brian?" John replied

"Well the shock of that machine exploding must have jolted her into being nice" Brian said in a sarcastic manner

"Yes your right" John said looking at Fiona

"I am always polite and as for being rude that's not me at all, I am sorry if I appeared so guys" Fiona said overwhelmed by their comments.

At that moment Alesha appeared on the ward and approached her bed

"Sorry about the incident in X ray I don't know what happened and I can only apologise about it" Alesha said appearing very tense.

"It's fine I am not injured in any way luckily" Fiona said in an understanding manner

"I will find out what happened and what the results are later" Alesha continued

"But I thought it may have failed to take anything" Fiona said watching Alesha fidgeting.

"Are you alright Alesha?" Fiona asked concerned

"Of course I am, just tired that's all" Alesha replied

She looked around the ward and noticed Fiona's visitors coming onto the ward Samantha and Elliot walked towards her.

"Now here's a our boss looking as radiant as usual" Elliot said smiling

"Flattery will get you everywhere Stuart"

"I ought to tell you she has had a bad experience" Alesha said "An accident in radiography but she is fine" Alesha explained "Some kind of electrical fault"

Samantha looked at her in surprise and then seemed to have flash backs of events from when she was at home with Elliot a few days ago. She remembered holding a knife over Elliot and wanting to kill him, she had cut herself in the process and still had a dressing on her hand as a form of reminder of the event. She seemed to visualise another incident where she was using a claw to injure Elliot as they were making love, this was not the type of things that Samantha did as a rule and so she considered it was a dream or even a nightmare. Samantha never engaged in sexual fantasies or sexual games of that nature she was rather straight laced and prudish by nature she was considered uneventful and boring in comparison with other people she was even reluctant to dress up. Naturally she was shocked by the images her mind had conjured up, but could not dismiss them from her mind.

"Stuart I feel strange and somewhat embarrassed by thoughts which have entered my head, the images won't go away as if they were real experiences" She said quietly to him.

"Procrastinating I call it, you have been like it for days ever since you attacked me, almost catatonic at times". Elliot said to her privately.

"Oh my god then it is all real?" Samantha said shocked

They returned to Fiona's bedside and acted as if nothing had happened, but Fiona could sense that something was wrong.

"Okay do you want to share your thoughts?" Fiona asked

"Well Samantha has undergone a personality change recently" Elliot said

"What more than usual?" Fiona said jokingly.

"No seriously Fi this is real" Samantha said bowing her head in shame.

"She was acting like Catherina did in a sexual way and tried to harm me" Elliot explained

"Even kill him" Samantha said

"Yes" Elliot thought for a moment "What?"

“I had a carving knife in my hand and went to stab him in the chest, I watched his chest rise while he was sleeping and wanted to stab him like he was a sacrificial lamb” Samantha did the motions.

“My god” Elliot said holding his chest

“So what stopped you? Fiona asked

“Fi!” Elliot exclaimed

“I don’t mean why didn’t you I mean what prevented you from killing him?” Fiona said correcting herself

“I love him and I would not want him to be harmed” Samantha admitted.

“Exactly your conscience and love for him saved him from death” Fiona was trying to rationalising the situation “Just as I didn’t attack those porters and yet I wanted to for some reason”

“You did?” Samantha said

“When did you start acting this way Sammy? Fiona asked

“Immediately after we left Mexico, or from the time we were in that volcano” Samantha replied realising what could have been the cause of her behaviour.

“And what about you Fi?” Elliot asked

"A few days ago I suppose, I didn't feel right and put it down to the accident" Fiona said

"I have felt fine for the last few days" Samantha said "like a weight has been lifted from my chest"

"I feel like that now, its like my body was taken over or like I was possessed or something" Fiona said looking at Samantha

"That could be it" Elliot said inspired by thought First you and then you he pointed to Samantha and then Fiona so who next" Elliot looked around and noticed Alesha was still close by treating another patient "That nurse maybe, cursed inside"

"Stuart, don't be ridiculous that's impossible how can that happen?" Samantha said dismissing his theory.

"Yes, come on Stuart be serious you know it's impossible, we deal with cold facts not fantasy" Fiona said agreeing with Samantha.

"Even so you know what we saw in that volcano with Zyanya and how did you become resurrected from the dead Sammy?" Elliot said trying to prove his point.

"I never died Stuart I was asleep" Samantha insisted

"You were clinically dead and that's a fact and I thought in the confusion that I noticed a kind of mist with a form of sparkling pieces of glass or some other substance enter your body via your mouth, it was weird. It was as if one of the mirrors had shattered into fragments of glass and travelled from the lake where Catherina had vanished in the lake of lava to you" Stuart said trying to search for answers to their dilemma.

"Stuart we do love you but you're completely crazy" Fiona said laughing

"Yes Stuart, you have been on something obviously" Samantha laughed with Fiona

"I don't know why I bother with you two, honestly I do try to come up with some kind of answer to your problem but you dismiss my theory, blow it out of the water". Elliot continued mumbling as Harrison entered the ward.

"Hi gang, tell me what have I missed?" Harrison asked cheerfully.

Back in the radiography department Dr Phillips points something out to Alison

"What is it?" Alison asks

"Something shiny in her chest" Dr Phillips describes what he sees on the X ray film "If I didn't know better I would say it was some kind of mirror"

"It looks like a face in it like something out of history" Alison says

"An Aztec face with some kind of head dress, very strange" Dr Phillips said intrigued

“Definitely something glass and we found fragments of glass on the floor” Alison said “Over where Fiona was lying”

“It could have been from the X ray equipment part of the debris from the explosion” Dr Phillips said searching for answers.

“No nothing travelled across there and it was by her neck sheltered from that side of the room” Alison said

“So the glass could be lodged in her chest, it still doesn’t explain why we see it as a mirror or in a solid mass” Dr Phillips said baffled.

“What are we going to do?” Alison asked concerned

“We need to keep this to ourselves until we know the answers” Dr Phillips insisted

But little did they know that Alesha was listening to their conversation hiding behind a door, she watched as Alison hid the X ray under some papers on her desk.

CURSE AND CONSEQUENCES

It was the early part of the evening when Fiona was asked to prepare for another X ray, Doctor Phillips had sent for her and Brian one of the porters appeared on the ward to assist her. Alesha looked particularly nervous and was pacing up and down near the nurses station, she looked across at Fiona and then left the ward ahead of them. She reached the radiography room and hid behind a door as she had done before, she waited for a while then produced a pair of long sharp scissors, then at the right moment she plunged them into Alison's back holding her other hand over Alison's mouth. Alison's eyes widen and Alesha stabbed her again making sure the long blade entered her lungs and that she would die. The Doctor came in and suffered the same fate his body fell into the next room and Alesha found another place to hide, hoping to catch Fiona and Brian by surprise having hid Alison's body under the table. But the porter wasn't alone his colleague John had appeared with another patient they were talking in the corridor, so Alesha decided to take the X ray and disappear through another door.

Fiona caught sight of her walking away up the corridor towards the lift, they all became distracted by Alison moaning inside the X ray room each one looked at the other then one of the porters looked in the room and soon returned.

"Alison has been stabbed, quick call for help" Brian shouted.

He returned to the room and then entered the second room.

"Christ Dr Phillips has been stabbed too" Brian went sheet white in the face his blood had drained out of his face and he was in shock.

Alesha ran from the hospital and hid near a rubbish bin, she removed a lighter from her pocket and set fire to the X ray film destroying any evidence of the mirror that lay inside the abdomen of Fiona. After this she ran out of the secluded area and into the street, it was then that she looked at her hands and noticed the blood. But before she had time to think a car travelled in her direction and knocked her to the ground, she lay helpless in the street noticing a crowd forming around her. One woman approached her offering to assist her, the woman gazed at her in a strange way, as if she were in a trance. She bowed her head down towards Alesha and glass fibre sprayed from Alesha's mouth into the woman's, causing her to gasp. The woman concerned had escaped from the hospital's psychiatric unit, she was a schizophrenic called Vanessa who was said to be very unstable, possibly of danger to herself and not others. Vanessa looked around then pushed her way though the crowd and ran down the street towards the railway station.

Vanessa boarded a late train heading to London, not many passengers boarded this particular train at this hour. She sat in the carriage for a while, she noticed a few passengers and one in particular who sat opposite her, he was a fat man with a bold head and wearing thick glasses. He began staring at her undressing her with his eyes, he was the kind of pervert that lady's usually tried to avoid like the plague.

"Are you travelling far" He asked a little breathless with excitement.

"Far enough thank you" Vanessa replied

"May I say you have a lovely face and figure" the man continued

"Thank you, but I am really not what I seem" Vanessa said hesitantly.

"Oh and what exactly do you mean, that you're a woman of mystery?" He joked

"Something like that, but you really don't want to know the real me" She warned

"Oh, but I do really" He insisted.

"I will be straight back I need to use the toilet" She excused herself.

"I will be waiting for you" He said smiling

Vanessa felt nauseous so she entered the toilet, holding her throat and coughing badly. She turned to face the mirror and became distressed, to her horror she saw a different face looking back at her. It was Catherina who was just as surprised seeing her and realising that Vanessa had noticed her she reacted by trying to alter her brain patterns, but all she managed to do was make her worse. Vanessa proceeded to vomit and produce worms from her mouth transforming into some kind of rotting corps with bloody eyes and a thin green looking skin. She fell backwards towards the wall and her form changed again looking like an hideous monster with razor sharp teeth and menacing eyes, she also had claws growing out of her fingers that once had chewed nails. She began roaring like a wild beast and left the toilet for the carriage where she had sat quietly. The passengers looked in horror at her appearance but never anticipated what was to follow, as Vanessa proceeded to attack the man first clawing him and tossing him into the air, and then she sent one of her claws straight through his eye penetrating his skull. Then she attacked each passenger in turn. She savagely tore at each one in frenzied manner scratching at them and tearing off limbs casting them aside. No one could escape as she speedily destroyed each person mercilessly until all of them were dead, then she wrote on one of the windows in blood 'cursed' She realised that she may have been caught by someone so she bit off her left hand and crawled under one of the bodies. There she lay until the train pulled into the next station leaving others to find the massacre in the carriage, with such an impossible story to tell. Forensics had tried to make sense of the carnage but with all the marks and bites they found nothing aboard that could match anything found on the bodies, but when they found Vanessa's body she had the DNA from each passenger on her. Catherina had left her body and entered the body of one of the forensic team making her escape casually walking away from the crime scene once more.

SEARCHING FOR HELP

At the hospital Fiona was finally discharged and made her way back to her apartment with her friends and colleagues. Harrison, Elliot and Samantha sat listening to Fiona discussing the hospital experience.

"I must confess, I am shocked by the murders in the hospital and then by Alesha's accident in the street, but then I here about a train massacre which is really beyond belief" Fiona said

"Such a lot has happened in a short space of time" Samantha commented.

"And you all still put it down to exact science and logic" Elliot said concerned "I think this goes back to Zyanya in Mexico"

“I agree!” Harrison shouted “We need answers and we can only get them in Mexico”

“Yes your right” Fiona said nodding

“My word I never saw that coming” Elliot said in surprise

“Why Stuart I may seem like a facts and figures lady but I really do think your right about Zyanya, she has the answers we need to find out more about the present curse, whatever that may be”. Fiona looked disturbed

“So who is going to go to Mexico?” Harrison asked

“Well I have a surprise for you” Fiona pointed to the door “Ruth, come inside”

Ruth Ashley the psychiatric nurse entered the room with her long hair flowing and her large eyes gazing around the room.

“Hello” She said smiling “Its so nice to see you all again”

Fiona greeted her with open arms as did Samantha, the men gave her a hug and then they all sat down and resumed their conversation.

“Ruth and Dan are going to Mexico to find Zyanya and seek a way of destroying Catherina and the curse while the rest of us find out more about the massacre on the train”.

“I may be wrong but I feel that I may be able to persuade Zyanya to help us” Ruth said confidently.

"So you do think that Catherina is responsible in some way?" Elliot asked

"There is a chance that from the way Sammy and I recall events that we may have been influenced by her in some way" Fiona said trying not to commit herself.

"That is sort of an admission for Fi, the closest you will get to her saying that we are all right about the possession thing. When in reality we all know that we have been possessed by her spirit and controlled by her to do things that are obviously out of character for us" Samantha explained.

"But at least you didn't commit murder" Elliot said

"I nearly killed you" Samantha said

"But you didn't" Elliot said

"No because your conscience never let you" Harrison said "That's the difference between you and the others, both Fiona and you would never kill anyone because your conscience stopped you".

"Yes, Alesha had a weaker mind and more susceptible to outer influences and Vanessa was a schizophrenic who was responding to both Catherina and her own mental state of mind, driven by this spirit and her own paranoia. You would have been confused by the hallucinations conjured up in her own thoughts and that of Christina's twisted personality, what a combination. No wonder she slaughtered all those people without a second thought". Ruth said hardly believing her own mind.

“So what a dilemma, we need to act fast in order to stop her” Harrison said looking at Fiona and then Ruth for support.

“So Dan go with Ruth and lets hope Zyanya will help us” Fiona said “I fear Ruth may be the main target as you helped Zyanya destroy Catherina”.

“I know this and I am happy to go to Mexico and sort this problem out” Ruth said bravely.

“I am happy to support you Ruth” Harrison said smiling.

“Then we will find out more from this end” Elliot said addressing Fiona and Samantha.

They all left the apartment and separated each heading in their own direction, Fiona went with Samantha, Ruth and Harrison went the same direction and Elliot continued in his own direction.

Ruth seemed quiet on the plane travelling over to Mexico with Harrison, the journey was long and boring for Ruth who was used to being occupied and active on the wards. Eleven and a half hours of flight doing nothing but watch in flight movies which just to piss Ruth off even more would be a disaster movie like airport about a plane disaster or towering inferno, but ultimately an annoying movie like final destination that had predictable scenes of carnage. Finally peace was shattered by a stewardess appearing with a smile and offer of some beverage which could have been served in the staff canteen given to a cat that would keel over and die. Ruth merely smiled back and politely accepted the coffee and free biscuits while Harrison was content with coffee and nuts. People walked down the aisle and joined an ever increasing cue for the toilet, it took forever for the cue to go down, and someone had obviously had some kind of stomach upset judging from the time factor and odious smell. Ruth found the hours of sitting observing others and watching movies so tedious that even the toilet situation was interesting, if only something really dramatic would happen like someone fainting or somebody opened the door in flight. But poor Ruth had to settle for a child vomiting into a bag which lasted all of fifteen minutes, the poor child was a sickly white colour and looked on her guardian for reassurance.

"It's alright Suzie you will be fine soon" Her mother said reassuringly.

"Okay Mum" She replied

Ruth smiled at the girl as if to also offer reassurance knowing exactly what it was like to be ill like this thinking back to the counselling days, which is not the best place to revisit thinking about the circumstances that lead to the counselling. Ruth had reflected many times on aspects of her past but tried to learn by her past experiences, eventually she became a stronger person and she felt that she was able to face anything. So did this mean that fear was a thing of the past, a non-existent thing or merely a dent in her armour. Do we ever go beyond fear into a false sense of security, is this what truly happens to people who have been abused?

Having survived the monotony of the eleven and a half hour journey Ruth and Harrison checked into a local hotel in close proximity to the volcano where they first met Zyanya. Ruth just wanted to explore while Harrison was more interested in drinking or what some people would call propping up the bar. Ruth toured the hotel and later walking down the streets looking into shops and quaint buildings, she didn't venture far from the hotel in case she got lost. Harrison went out to meet her concerned about her safety, but Ruth reassured him that she was safe and able to defend herself.

"Dan it is kind of you to show concern but I can handle myself" Ruth said smiling

"Well I just wanted to make sure Ruth" Harrison said concerned

"Dan really I have challenged the world and even asked a witch called Zyanya for help, do you think anything from this street can affect me?"

No sooner had these words left her mouth than a loud bang occurred like the sound of a powerful gun or a car back firing. In fact it was the sound of a door slamming shut, Ruth jumped and clung hold of Harrison.

"Well that certainly affected you" Harrison said laughing.

Ruth pulled away from him "Very funny Dan" She slapped him on the arm and laughed.

They walked back to the hotel arm in arm watching activities all around them, Ruth was fascinated by the way the people were dressed and interacted in their native language, she understood some Spanish but only enough to order food or ask directions. She did not anticipate a full conversation about anything in particular, Harrison was fluent in Spanish and Italian so when it came to arranging a trip to the ancient Aztec ruins he spoken in Spanish in order for clarification of the prearranged journey's or program. But their main interest was returning to the volcano and persuading Zyanya to help them defeat Catherina, They reached the area of land which was a desert terrain with a small woodland area, a pathway led to the volcano that had a small opening leading into the area where they left Zyanya resting in a lake. Ruth and Harrison walked on the deserted rough dirt path at a steady pace until they reached the entrance to the volcano, it was concealed by bushes that they had left on their last trip. They began to pull them away piece by piece until they revealed the opening, Ruth entered first brushing away cob webs as they walked along a dark passage. Harrison grabbed a torch from the wall and lit it, while Ruth took a battery operated one from her bag.

"Will this do?" She asked smiling.

"I really never thought of that Ruth" Harrison replied sarcastically

"Well that's not all I have in the way of gadgets" Ruth said

"I bet" Harrison replied looking her up and down

"Now Dan remember who I am" Ruth swiftly replied

“Ruth Ashley” He said without a moment’s thought.

“I was referring to my sexuality not my name” Ruth explained “Or was that your feeble attempt at sarcasm?”

“I do assure you Ruth I am aware that you are a lesbian, but like most men would say it is a waste of a good looking woman”. Harrison said gazing at her.

“Some ladies would argue with that, saying your loss their gain” Ruth cleverly replied.

“Seriously though Ruth I do admire your constitution fighting for what you believe and defending your cause, just like I admire and respect your courage.

“Why thank you Daniel, I must say I admire your bravery”

“Me, I am only as brave as the next man or woman” He said looking ahead of him into the darkness”.

But what really lay beyond the darkness, was it the dark and solitary place that Ruth was used to or something more sinister than both of them could ever imagine. Soon the answer would appear before them and put them both on the defensive, but what kind of vision could cause them to tremble and shake with fear. Suddenly a loud roar was heard coming from the darkness this was followed by slimy creatures falling from the walls and above their heads, both Ruth and Harrison dodged most of these. Unfortunately some dropped on them making Ruth scream and Harrison yell out, but both of them moved forward aware of the pending dangers ahead. This was evidently Zyanya protecting herself and her magic from outside intruders, she was insistent that she never wanted uninvited guests entering her dwelling and that included Ruth and Harrison. They reached the lake and the ground began to rumble, a snake appeared first and then vanished this was replaced by a large panther roaring at them. They both stopped in their tracks and gazed into his yellow eyes and then at his sharp teeth it was sat on a rock, then they heard a roar from behind them, both turned to see another panther behind them. Both panthers began pacing and then leapt towards them with their front claws facing them, sticking out in order to attack them. Was this the end of Ruth and Harrison both of them thought so as they grabbed each other and closed their eyes?

Suddenly everything went quiet followed by a rumbling and the lake began to bubble up and the area became very hot with fire rising into the air like fireworks. From the centre of the lake a figure arose dressed in Aztec clothing, a flowered head dress and clothes decorated with golden designs and emblems in the shape of birds. She held a staff with the head of a snake that came to life as she did, she was angry and appeared to spit fire at them.

"Why do you come here when you know that you will die?" She shouted

Harrison walked forward "We need your help!" he said

Zyanya sent a fireball in his direction and knocked him to the ground

"Zyanya mighty witch, why do you attack us when we come for your help?" Ruth said rushing to rescue Harrison.

"Silence child you dare to return when I told you not to" Zyanya said angrily

"What happened to the merciful forgiving Zyanya who once helped us?" Ruth asked crouching over Harrison's body.

"How dare you be so insolent child, do you know I can destroy you in the blink of an eye?" Zyanya seemed to get larger as she grew angrier.

"So why don't you do it after all you had the reputation of being an evil witch who cursed people and hated everyone, fucking bring it on witch?" Ruth replied angrily

"Why do you goad me child when it means you will die?" Zyanya said confused

"Because I have been to hell and back and faced a fucking world of evil so all you will do is end all that, so I would be glad to die" Ruth replied boldly.

Zyanya began to calm down and even showed signed of smiling as if she had mellowed, Ruth watched as she made all the creatures around her disappear. Harrison opened his eyes and was astonished by Zyanya as she appeared in a human form next to them.

"Never has anyone challenged me like you, what is your name?" Zyanya asked.

"Ruth Ashley" Ruth replied confidently

"Then Ruth Ashley, how may I help you?" Zyanya said clasping her had

"Catherina is after us she sends a curse to all who had her destroyed here at the volcano" Ruth explained "She is evil"

"So Catherina lives after all" Zyanya said pondering.

"Yes, she wants to avenge her own death" Ruth continued "She had killed many innocent people" Ruth said excitedly.

"Tut tut Ruth Ashley I will help you" Zyanya smiled "The question is how"

"I have no idea Zyanya" Ruth said smiling back

"You are indeed a brave girl and I admire your courage so I will think of something" Zyanya looked at Harrison "I remember him he was about to be sacrificed and you helped save him"

"I merely spoke to you pleading for his life" Ruth said modestly.

"But you showed no fear as you repeated today, you are somewhat like me" Zyanya explained thinking back to her life.

Harrison still appeared stunned by his fireball experience, but seemed to take in most of the conversation. "So what happens now?"

"Do you know where Catherina is?" Zyanya asked

"She is constantly possessing human bodies in order to carry out her evil plan, she was last reported to be on a train where she massacred a carriage of passengers showing no mercy" Ruth explained

"So, mind manipulation and uses bodies for a short time as the human tissue is unable to sustain the energy that her body omits" Zyanya explained "She will prove to be quite a challenge I must confess".

"But you will be able to stop her?" Harrison asked

"Hopefully with Ruth's help" Zyanya said confidently.

"How will you travel with us?" Ruth asked

"Well I will need your body later so I suppose his body will have to do" Zyanya said pointing to Harrison.

"Oh god" Harrison said a little apprehensively.

"Don't worry no harm will come to you" Zyanya reassured him "It is just for transportation purposes".

Zyanya transformed into a small glowing red substance like a cloud of powder and vanished into Harrison's mouth, he seemed to go into a trance and then appeared normal until he spoke.

"Shall we go?" Zyanya said through Harrison

“Your voice” Ruth said “You sound like Zyanya”

“Well, it is me” She replied “Should I sound like him?” Zyanya asked.

“Well, it would be more credible to be honestly” Ruth said shocked.

“Is this better” came Harrison’s male deep voice

“Yes that’s more like Dan” Ruth was still puzzled “Is Dan in there, I mean functional and does he know what’s going on?

“He lies dormant and can sense some of the things happening, he can also prevent me from using him to hurt others” Zyanya explained

“Catherina must have found people who were already psychopaths in order to use them in her massacre on the train, weak or mad people that could be manipulated” Ruth tried to fathom things out in her mind.

They all set out and returned to the hotel, Zyanya gazed around the room.

“Things have changed since my day, what is that thing?” Zyanya asked

“A television set, it transmits shows and movies to everyone’s home” Ruth explained then went onto explain about other facilities and appliances knowing that she would ask about them.

"I need to use the bathroom" Zyanya explained heading for the elegant bathroom

"How do I do this" she asked

Ruth realised her dilemma being in a male body and never seeing a modern toilet like the one in the hotel. She explained the best she could but started to tie herself in knots trying to explain it all.

Ruth advised her to sit on it although men usually stood to urinate and sit to have a bowel action, this took some explaining "Just sit" she advised. Ruth had to orientate Zyanya in a lot of things, teach her about the twenty first century in no time at all. Ruth loved a challenge but this was far beyond this, she needed to explain about transportation and all the other subsequent changes that would affect Zyanya. But actually experiencing these things were different, after all she would need to experience these things for herself in order to fully appreciate the modern age.

The next big challenge was the airport terminal and flying to England on that long journey home, an experience that is problematic even for a modern woman like Ruth.

"How long will it take for this floating metal to reach are destination?" Zyanya asked

"Eleven and a half hours from now" Ruth explained

"That's a long time?" Zyanya asked "Try eternity"

Ruth found the return journey more tolerable talking to Zyanya, she seemed very interesting and discussed many things past and present. She also explained a little about how she planned to defeat Catherina inside the body of Ruth, this was quite disturbing for Ruth as she felt the one who was being attacked. Eventually they landed in England and travelled back to Ruth's apartment where they met their friends and began planning their next move. Catherina continued to leave devastation in her pathway and managed to make news headlines with further murders, although she managed to keep her identity secret. Fiona knew who was behind the train massacre and other incidents in the area, Christina was preparing for her attack on Ruth and others who helped to destroy her in the volcano in Mexico.

THE FINAL BATTLE

There was calm in the air on the evening when all was expected to happen, Ruth and Harrison had returned, the spirit of Zyanya remained inside Harrison. But her spirit was resting while Harrison gathered his wits and began conversing with his friends and colleagues discussing the pending battle of the spirits. Ruth seemed anxious pacing up and down and becoming quite sharp with her friends, she was frightened and nothing could change her feelings of anxiety. She had been abused and remembered how that felt as a child confining herself in a wardrobe as her solitude of safety, but this time she was unable to hide from danger like the time she faced her abusers. She fought them mentally, demonstrating her inner strength and came out stronger for her efforts. But this was different she was fighting a spirit a mighty opponent who could destroy her or her friends without mercy, did she have the strength to defeat her even if she was just the host body for Zyanya. But Zyanya chose he for her mental strength and courage which she admired in Ruth. A woman who could battle fearlessly until the end, a person who would never allow anyone to beat her, Ruth considered this and began to calm down.

“Bring it on Catherina I am ready for you” Ruth shouted

Fiona and Harrison were apprehensive they knew that Ruth would be the main target Samantha was nervous and clung hold of Elliot, she hardly spoke but her eyes expressed so much. It took a while for someone to actually speak that evening Zyanya had made her presence known to Catherina who had been searching for them, particularly Ruth who she considered the main cause of her death.

Samantha broke the silence by banging a mug on the table and shouting.

“This is impossible, are we sure that she are coming?” Samantha looked around at her friends.

“Yes Zyanya said she is definitely coming” Ruth replied

“I fucking hate this waiting” Samantha continued

“Sam we all hate this waiting” Ruth said trying to remain calm

“So how do you think she will make her entrance” Fiona asked

“Well she won’t knock the door and wait” Elliot said sarcastically

"Stuart you tosser" Samantha said frowning at him "Was that necessary"

"I suppose not" Elliot replied

"Now let's not get nasty vent your anger towards the enemy" Fiona advised

No sooner had these words left Fiona's mouth that they heard Ruth's apartment door bang open taking the door completely off its hinges, the door landed on the other side of the hallway and a creature appeared with yellow eyes and scaly skin. She rushed into the lounge area by this time Zyanya had transferred into Ruth's body and looked similar to the invading creature.

Catherina began to do battle by hurling fire balls at each of the observers, this was counteracted by a wall of ice that Zyanya produced to protect them. Then both of them transformed as snakes and proceeded to fight each other, spitting, hissing and entwining their bodies around each other. They bit each other and fought wildly around the room until they transformed into dragons and then back to their human hosts. The wounds appeared on the host bodies Ruth had cuts and bites on her.

"Separate her from the mirror that is protecting her" Zyanya shouted

"But how do we do this?" Fiona asked desperately

"Gather up all the mirrors as I told you before and form a circle around us" Zyanya shouted.

They all collected mirrors for other room's and formed a circle as instructed, other friends had joined them by this time including Ruth's sister Claire. Suddenly the mirror left Catherina host and shattered, it disappeared and Catherina left her host body and became a black panther Zyanya left Ruth's body and also became a wild cat they leapt at each other and went flying out of the window like a storm. Glass shattered everywhere and it was almost like a large explosion as they fell into the street both transforming into hideous monsters. Ruth was helped up by Samantha while the others attended to the other host body who was a young girl, she looked bewildered and looked around her confused.

"You are safe now" Fiona said

"Why am I here?" She asked

"We will explain later, I am Fiona" Fiona introduced her friends too

"I am Tanya" She said looking at her wounds "What the fuck has happened to me?"

"Come with us and see for yourself" Samantha said leading everybody outside

The battle of the spirits continued as both spirits drifted towards the park, they were sending bolts of lighting towards each other, everybody watched from a safe distance. Ruth still felt in danger as she watched the savage attacks of both spirits, Tanya was astonished by the sight of these creatures fighting before her. Neither monsters weakened and the fight went on, but then Catherina turned on Ruth and began throwing flaming missiles at her Samantha used her body to protect her and was badly injured Harrison also tried to protect her and also fell wounded. Zyanya had vanished and the crowd thought she had been destroyed; she was no where in sight while Catherina took Ruth and held her up in the air.

"See your friend Ruth and watch her perish" Catherina shouted "I will pull her apart and send you the pieces" Catherina began pulling at Ruth causing her to yell out.

"Leave my sister alone!" Claire shouted running towards the creature

Catherina kicked her out of the way and caught Claire with her claw, stabbing her in the stomach, Claire fell to the ground in agony. Blood began to seep through her clothes and Fiona ran to her aid but felt helpless as she watched Claire fade away and die. Catherina hoped that Ruth would see this before she tore her body apart, Catherina's eye began to get brighter and were shining in the darkness. She was about to pull Ruth apart like play dough but she was suddenly hit by a bolt of lightening projected by Zyanya's mighty hand. The force caused her to drop Ruth to the ground, she was stunned for a while watching Catherina fall back also shaken by the impact of the lightening. Ruth gathered her wits and ran as fast as she could towards Claire, she then sat sobbing holding her limp body, then partly through rage and for the love of Claire she shouted out.

"You fucking murdering bitch!" Ruth shook her fist at her.

Fiona tried to console her by wrapping her arms around her, but Ruth pushed her away and got herself up. Ruth proceeded to run back towards Catherina with the branch of a tree.

"Come on fucking bitch bring it on, fight me" Ruth said trusting the branch into her leg, Catherina yelled out.

Zyanya was shocked at Ruth's actions and noticed that somehow it had affected Catherina, she noticed that she was getting weaker and took advantage by striking her over and over again. Before long others joined in the fight by also getting branches and stabbing her.

"I am the witch queen Zyanya not you" Christina said trying to gather up strength

"No Christina, you have no compassion, no power and will die trying to defeat me" Zyanya said striking her once more.

Finally Zyanya produced so much power she created a golden spear and threw it into the air like a javelin, it travelled through the air at great speed and penetrated Catherina's chest causing her to fall back and land on the ground with a mighty thump. Catherina's body vanished leaving Zyanya to face a large crowd of people, she took advantage of this moment to exercise her power and wisdom.

"Today you have witnessed the power of good over evil, I bring back whoever has been harmed back to health by my magic as Zyanya the witch. Let this be a lesson to anyone who uses a curse to destroy people. No one has the god forsaken right to hurt anyone else whether from abuse of any kind or wickedness, love one another and be at peace with mankind. Let no woman. No child suffer but help each other to get through life by demonstrating love and understanding to everyone, we are all equal and must be respected for our own individual personalities and sexuality, may your god bless you amen".

With these words Zyanya vanished and the crowd disbursed leave Ruth to gaze around at her friends, and then she noticed Claire standing up and rushing towards her.

"Claire!" Ruth shouted with delight

"Ruth your alive" Claire said hugging her

"Thank you friends for fighting with me" Ruth said smiling

Ruth had been through so much in her life but nothing could compare with this event, she was so shocked by what she had seen as were some of the spectators. Police ambulance and fire crew were bewildered and could offer no explanation for the sight that they had witnessed many questions were asked but all the evidence had disappeared, there was no trace of any spiritual battle everything had been cleared up. It was as if a mass hallucination had taken place Zyanya had turned everything back to normal before disappearing.

They all went back to Ruth's tidy apartment nobody wanting to admit that they saw anything, so had this been an hallucination shared by all or was there more to this story. Make your own mind up but consider this point, the history is real the scars remain outside and inside Ruth and Claire discovered this. Also before the night ended Zyanya reappeared as the Aztec witch and said.

"Can I borrow someone's body to get me home?

MYSTERY OF THE RACADIA

The team of investigators from criminal world investigate the mystery of the Racadia, a cruise ship where people go missing. Fiona, Samantha, Harrison and Elliot board the ship from Southampton as passengers while Pavina enrols as a waitress, Ruth Ashley and her sister Claire board the ship in Belgium and the adventure begins. The first suspect is an illusionist who is part of the entertainment crew, but further clues seem to lead to other suspects as the mystery continues on the Racadia.

OPERATION
BRAINSTORM
Simon Robert Sinclair

FURTHER READING

CRACKED PORCELAIN ACTS OF ABUSE
(Trilogy) one, two and three

CRACKED PORCELAIN- THE FULL STORY

CRACKED PORCELAIN- THE FULL STORY TWO

BROKEN WINGS AND LOST SOULS

CRACKED PORCELAIN- THE FULL STORY THREE

REMEMBER ME

DOUBLE EXPOSURE

STORIES BEYOND BELIEF

CONFLICT OF FAITH

ULTIMATE PURPOSE

FOR THE LOVE OF CHARLOTTE

THE HARRINGTON CURSE

CURSE OF ZYANYA

Contact sarahruthscott3@gmail.com or visit me on Facebook